S0-AVS-469

DEMOLITION DERBY

They are auto workers, streaming from the goddamn plant, before the three o'clock whistle stops. They can't get away fast enough.

The youngbloods come first, eager to kick ass, yelling as they dash across the huge parking lot to their Mustangs and Camaros. Jumping in, they gun supercharged motors and spit gravel, honking and revving, cutting off everybody, struggling to be the first through the gate . . .

Suddenly the roaring traffic jam erupts onto Route 41 and races flat out down the busy highway. The thundering car pack does ninety plus in the twenty-five zone, speeding so crazily they make the Indy 500 seem like slot cars.

Drivers often die less than a mile from the plant. But nobody cares. Hell, they're dying anyway. At least death on the road is uncertain or fast. Death at the goddamn plant is both certain and slow.

RICHARD PRYOR
HARVEY KEITEL
YAPHET KOTTO

In

BLUE COLLAR

With
CLIFF DeYOUNG

Written by
PAUL SCHRADER & LEONARD SCHRADER

Directed by
PAUL SCHRADER

Produced by
DON GUEST

Executive Producer
ROBIN FRENCH

Music by
JACK NITZSCHE

A
T.A.T. COMMUNICATIONS COMPANY PRODUCTION

A
UNIVERSAL RELEASE

BLUE COLLAR

A novel by
Leonard Schrader

Based on the screenplay
by Paul Schrader
and Leonard Schrader

BLUE COLLAR
A Bantam Book / March 1978

*Cover photographs courtesy MCA Publishing, A division of
MCA, Inc.*

All rights reserved.
*Cover photograph copyright © 1977 by Universal City Studios,
Inc.*
*Copyright © 1978 by Paul Schrader and Leonard Schrader.
This book may not be reproduced in whole or in part, by
mimeograph or any other means, without permission.
For information address: Bantam Books, Inc.*

ISBN 0-553-11869-2

Published simultaneously in the United States and Canada

*Bantam Books are published by Bantam Books, Inc. Its trade-
mark, consisting of the words "Bantam Books" and the por-
trayal of a bantam, is registered in the United States Patent
Office and in other countries. Marca Registrada, Bantam
Books, Inc., 666 Fifth Avenue, New York, New York 10019.*

PRINTED IN THE UNITED STATES OF AMERICA

For Pelepone

Ford's will hire anything. What they really want are chimpanzees.
—CELINE

Unions were born to help keep the bosses off your back, but today they help the bosses screw you.
—AUTO WORKER

1

In the 1920s they came to Detroit like pretty girls to Hollywood. In the 1970s they felt bored, brutalized, exhausted, angry. Most hated their jobs. Many hated their lives.

They were auto workers, streaming from the goddamn plant before the three o'clock whistle stopped. They couldn't get away fast enough. No more ass-busting, no more ass-kissing. They wanted out.

The youngbloods came first, eager to kick ass, yelling as they dashed across the huge parking lot to their Mustangs and Camaros. Jumping in, they gunned supercharged motors and spit gravel for the gate, braking only to avoid major collisions. "Get outa my face, mutha!" Each driver honked and revved, cutting off everybody, struggling to be first through the gate.

The lifers came next, eager to rest their bones, lunch buckets dangling from their weary hands. They trudged toward their reliable Datsuns and Buicks, dodging the hot rods careening wildly toward the bottleneck at the gate. "Damn punks." Reaching their cars, they plunked down behind steering wheels and waited for the demolition derby to finish.

A pinstriped Corvette suddenly sideswipe-crashed into a customized GTO. Neither driver backed off an inch. Tromping on the gas, they stutter-gunned forward, metal screeching, grinding their mangled new cars against each other.

The first car through the gate, driven by a young black, was a battered new T-Bird with hand-painted words along the side: *I Love a White Woman.*

Suddenly the roaring traffic jam erupted onto Route 41 and raced flat out down the busy highway. The thundering car pack did ninety plus in the twenty-five zone, speeding so crazily they made the Indy 500 seem like slot cars.

Drivers often died less than a mile from the plant. But nobody cared. Hell, they were dying anyway. At least death on the road was uncertain or fast. Death at the goddamn plant was both certain and slow.

Three miles later, the factories were replaced by roadside taverns. The drivers skidded into the dirt parking lots and hopped out of their banged-up cars laughing.

"Wheee! You can't lose with the stuff I use."

Oogie's Bar & Grill was like a thousand taverns near a thousand factories. It had what mattered most: no foreman, no family, no bullshit.

"Par-ty, par-ty!"

The workers pushed through the door into Happy Hour. Some rushed straight to the bar, while others crowded around the pool table and pinball machines. The jukebox belted out a Nashville lament on the puzzling journey "From Barrooms to Bedrooms."

"Hey, Oog!"

"Set 'em up, Doris."

The noisy crowd was racially integrated, but more from convenience than choice. Working with a man made it seem stupid to refuse a drink with him. Yet while seeming to mingle, the whites and blacks stayed mostly with their own kind, as if there was an unwritten code against any real mixing.

Zeke Brown, Jerry Bartowski, and Smokey James didn't give a damn. They were the only group that broke the code.

Other workers viewed them with envy and fear, not really knowing what to make of them. Sure, the three crazy bastards could be the life of the party, but messing with the unwritten code was asking for trouble. Everybody knew that. At best they were crazy jokers trying to kick ass, but at worst just dumb suckers headed for the pits. In any case, keep some distance. Guys like that could be killers. They didn't know where to stop. They could make you lose your job, even your goddamn life—and for what?

Zeke, Jerry, and Smokey strolled through the

doorway into Oogie's Bar & Grill. They had little in common except for blue-collar work clothes and a two-word philosophy of life: fuck off.

They greeted the crowd and took the only vacant table in the middle of the room. Some workers taunted them, others asked to join them, but nobody ever took that table before they arrived—it was *theirs*.

Zeke Brown was a lightning bolt. Thirty-one, lanky and sly, he was an urban-bred black who didn't know where he would strike next. His quick eyes never missed a trick. Though his devilish smile promised madcap excitement, his wiry body emitted a restless energy in search of power. He wanted to rip off the whole system for anything possible, or at least his fair share. But he never did, because he was everybody's scapegoat: an assembly worker with a wife and five kids.

Jerry Bartowski was a clenched fist. Thirty-two, stocky and brash, he was a street-wise white guy who didn't know what he wanted to hit. His steady gaze never trusted anything. Though his pensive face promised loyalty, his tight muscular body emitted an impatient energy in search of revenge. He wanted nothing more than for the whole system—government, company, union—to leave him alone. But they never did, because he was everybody's victim: a spot-welder with a wife and two kids.

Smokey James was a cold mountain. Thirty-six, sullen and huge, he was a black ex-convict who rarely spoke. His hulking frame and steely eyes did his talking for him. He spent all his pay entertaining women friends, but never had a steady girl because that required a belief in the future that he didn't have. If he wanted anything, it was for the system to attack him in the open. But he knew they never would, because he was everybody's nemesis: a utility man without family or friends. He had what he wanted—nothing.

"Get it on, Doris," Zeke yelled, slamming his palm on the table. "My motor needs gasoline."

"Shit, take more than gasoline to start *your* motor," she said, plunking down three bottles of Stroh's beer. "You need to be overhauled."

"Say what, bitch?" Zeke grinned and made as if aiming a shotgun. "I can overhaul your ragged old ass in my sleep. Give you a Dee-troit dee-vorce."

"Shit," she chuckled, extending her hand for payment.

A clean-cut bystander handed her a ten-dollar bill, saying "It's on me." The three men eyed him suspiciously. Who the shit was this guy? His work clothes were unstained, his arms unscarred.

John Burrows sat down, saying, "Mind if I ask some questions?"

"Not if you're paying," Jerry muttered, sipping his beer.

"You guys work at the plant, right?"

Zeke flashed his cynical smile. "Just till times get better, Jack. Normally we all work on Wall Street."

"Well, I'm an instructor at Eastern Michigan. I'm doing my doctoral thesis on the union movement in Detroit. I wanted to ask you about Bald Eddie. Is he—?"

"Forget it, Jack," Zeke interrupted. "Be easier getting into virgin pussy."

Jerry nodded. "Nobody fucks with Bald Eddie."

Before Burrows could resume, Zeke had figured out a way to put him on, and said, "Hey, what's this *thesis* shit? Is that some sex-research jive?"

"No, not exactly. It's—"

"I hear some dudes be getting paid for fucking. Is that shit true?"

"I wouldn't know about that."

"Damn, Jack, I been researching pussy all my life. I mean searching and re-searching, and I never been paid shit."

"It's not exactly my field. You see, I—"

"And Smokey here, he's such a pussyhound that he be a professional. You ever been paid for it, Smoke?"

"Shit," Smokey muttered.

Burrows threw up his hands and stopped trying to ask them questions. Zeke leaned back, sipping his beer with a satisfied smile. Jerry grinned and said, "Don't let these fuck-offs bother you. What do you want?"

"Well, who's your union rep?"

"Clarence Hill."

"The muthafucker," Zeke muttered bitterly, the mere mention of the name changing his mood completely.

Seizing this opportunity, Burrows returned to his initial topic. "Is Bald Eddie still in touch with the men? I mean, he was a real ballbuster when he came up, but that was thirty years ago."

Still bitter, Zeke said, "Fuckers are all the same, Jack."

Jerry nodded. "They've been eating on too many tables with tablecloths."

"Take young guys on the line today, like you—"

"Bullshit," Smokey suddenly said, having been studying Burrows with cold intensity. "That honky ain't no college instructor."

Jerry was surprised: "Huh?" But the guilty look on Burrows' stunned face showed that Smokey had hit the mark again.

"That honky ain't no college nothing. I know his face. He work for the F.B.I."

"You're crazy," said Burrows, recovering quickly. "I've got nothing to do with the police."

"I've seen your face," said Smokey, looking away. Once he'd confirmed his suspicion, he didn't care anymore.

"I'm just an instructor," said Burrows, appealing to Zeke and Jerry. "I wanted to ask some questions. You've got nothing to be ashamed of, do you?"

"Ashamed!" Jerry jumped to his feet, angry he hadn't spotted an impostor, more angry an outsider was knocking his union. "Listen, asshole, we went out three years ago for seventy-two fucking days and I was on the picket line every day, and I'm still paying the goddamn bills for the money I borrowed to support my family. And you know what, asshole, we got our raise. I'm proud of my union and ain't no college shitface gonna make me say different."

Not to be outdone, Zeke stood and opened his shirt to reveal the scar on his chest. "I got nothin' to hide, mutha."

"Get that on the job?"

"*These* from the job, mutha." Zeke thrust out his badly scarred forearms, then pointed to the scar tissue twisting across his chest. "*This* from when the pigs attacked me on the picket line."

Doris arrived with another round of beer. Jerry whispered in Zeke's ear, "I thought you got that from that crazy Dolores bitch on River Street." As they sat down, Zeke mumbled, "Same thing, sucker."

"So tell me," said Burrows. "Why do you let your union rip you off as much as management? Do you *like* getting fucked over?"

That tore it for Jerry. Jumping back to his feet, he raised his fist. Hell, he knew he was getting fucked over. Sure, the union was the company's goddamn business partner. Sure, the union screwed the workers. Sure, the union treated them like second-class shit. But what the hell, the union was all they had. Sometimes it even helped.

"Get your ass outa here." Jerry pointed his fist at Burrows. "You don't know shit. You goddamn phony-baloney professor."

"All right by me," said Burrows, standing up and shrugging. "Ain't *my* kids who can't have new shoes, ain't *my* wife who—"

"That's fighting words, motherfucker." Zeke stood up slowly, lifting his beer bottle like a club. It was bad enough for some sucker to chop his union, but absolutely nobody ever said nothing about his family, especially no honky.

Burrows took a step toward the door, glancing around for help. Smokey grinned coldly. Zeke and Jerry edged forward, moving around the table for an all-out attack if he didn't back down.

Doris, still holding the beer, said, "Who's gonna pay for these?"

Jerry glanced at Zeke and Smokey. They all knew beers weren't free. Then he pointed at Burrows: "He ordered 'em."

"But I've been told to leave."

"So stay," Jerry relented. "Just don't talk about my union. Now pay for the beers."

"Plus the next two rounds," said Zeke. "That's nine bottles, Doris."

Burrows hesitated at Zeke's obvious put-down. Smokey stood up, towering over Burrows, and glared down into his face: "Pay for the beer, boy."

Burrows handed Doris the money.

The three workers took a Stroh's from her tray, then glanced at each other and nodded. They strolled over to the pinball machines without looking back, sipping the beer, leaving Burrows abandoned and alone at their empty table.

Burrows pocketed his change and watched them, especially Jerry. He'd been right. Nothing was crazier than working all your life for zilch, but these three were crazy enough to try anything. Maybe he'd finally found his man.

Eight hours later Zeke Brown lay conked out on his living-room sofa. He'd been asleep for two hours with a beer can in his hand. Carolyn, his attractive wife, turned off the TV and approached him.

She smiled sympathetically at the sprawling weary figure, grateful he wasn't an alcoholic. Everybody knew auto workers were never drunks, because drunks couldn't hold a job. But there were only two kinds of auto workers: those who drank a lot, and those who drank a helluva a lot. She was glad he only drank a lot.

"Come on, Zeke."

Helping him to his feet, she assisted him down the hallway. Suddenly the pain shot up his neck. He stumbled against the wall, clutching his forehead.

She winced, trying to stay calm: "Is it your eyes, honey?"

"No, just dizzy."

He staggered into the bedroom and collapsed on the bed, burying his face in the pillow as if it would make the world go away.

Removing his shirt, Carolyn caressed his smooth back and began massaging his muscular shoulders. She tried not to worry, even though she still didn't know why her father had gone blind. One doctor said it might be the lead in his blood, since he'd painted cars at Chrysler for twenty-six years. But Workmen's Comp refused to pay a penny. All the union did was recommend a lawyer, and all the lawyer got him was Medicaid—not even Unemployment. Everybody knew it was cheaper for the company to compensate cripples and widows than to install safety measures, but what they didn't know was that the company wouldn't even pay the compensation. All she knew was that Zeke had to get off the line before it killed him. And that if he was white, he would've had a promotion by now.

Jerry Bartowski trudged into his bedroom at one-thirty. Arlene, his good-looking wife, was waiting in bed. He yanked off his clothes and collapsed on the mattress beside her.

Arlene pulled the blanket over his abdomen and thighs, then caressed his powerful shoulders, but he didn't respond. She kissed the faded high school tattoo on his arm. He just stared blankly at the ceiling.

"Your back still hurts, don't it, honey?"

"Mmm."

"The school nurse called today. She says Debby's gotta have those teeth braces."

"Ar-*lene*," he muttered with an irritated sigh.

"I'm just trying to warn you, Jerry. She's gonna ask you for them again. She's getting up early to make your breakfast."

Jerry placed his forearm across his eyes as if it would blot out the whole world. He had to get up in four hours. He wanted to forget everything—the braces he couldn't afford, the bills he couldn't pay, and mostly the assembly line he couldn't avoid in another five hours.

Arlene snuggled next to him. She hated upsetting him when he looked so worn out. But it was her only chance, since he'd started working four nights a week at the gas station. And even with the extra money, they still couldn't pay all the bills. At least if they were black, they could get welfare or something.

2

TAKE-HOME PAY: $190 a week, $9,880 a year.
THE ASSEMBLY LINE: 4,400 cars a week, 220,000 a
year.
WORKING CONDITIONS: 8 hours a shift, plus 30 minutes for lunch, with 5 minutes an hour to run
for a quick Coke or a quick piss.

At daybreak the auto workers plodded across the huge parking lot with their heads down. They were convicts on the honor system, voluntarily returning to prison after an overnight pass.

Shortly before the six-thirty whistle, most workers shuffled inside the plant. But some suddenly dashed back to their cars and sped away. Sometimes they couldn't eat their daily shit, no matter what the price.

The torture chamber was darker than a subway

tunnel, hotter than a desert, louder than artillery. Heavy machinery shook the foundations, the air was thick with poison fumes, the steamy heat soared over 145 degrees.

They strained and hustled all along the line, young men with headbands working beside old women with hairnets, lean-faced blacks with Afros beside wrinkle-faced whites with crew cuts. Arms moving, legs moving, they pushed metal parts into place: fenders, trunks, floor pans. Always moving, they swung and fired the staccato power guns suspended from electric cords: power drills, power chisels, power wrenches. Moving, moving, they made a car a minute, 55 cars an hour.

Dogshit Miller, the foreman, stalked down the line. Pointing his beefy arms at offenders, he barked out his litany in tune with the clanging machines.

"Move it, Terry. . . . Get off your butt, Franklin. . . . Keep her rolling, boys! No slackers on *this* line!"

Zeke Brown worked glue-and-rubber on windshields. Every sixty seconds, he lifted a windshield from the stack, smeared glue all around the edge, and forced a rubber sleeve over the glued edge. He lifted the sleeved windshield and attached it to suction cups on the hydraulic lift, then he started to glue-and-rubber all over again.

Chicken Salad O'Neill, the hunchbacked old worker standing beside him, operated the hydraulic lift. He swung the windshield over the line, lowered it onto the passing car frame, and waited for two workers to remove it. Then he hurried back to Zeke for the next one.

Chicken Salad did "easy work," because he

couldn't work at all. His spine had been permanently damaged on the job. But he hadn't discovered the injury until he got home, so the company refused compensation by maintaining it was a bowling injury. After twenty-one years on the line, they gave him the choice of "easy work" or nothing. He vented his anger by mumbling incessantly. With each movement of his body, he mumbled, "Sumabitch . . . sumabitch . . ."

By ten o'clock every morning Zeke needed cotton balls to stop the bleeding in his nose. Every week for seven months he'd filed a formal complaint about the ventilation system. He'd stopped because Clarence Hill said the union couldn't do anything, but mostly because Dogshit Miller threatened to put him back on "dirty work"—where first-degree burns and broken bones were not so much a matter of luck, but a matter of time.

On top of everything else, Zeke had re-cut his finger on his broken locker. If it wasn't getting infected from the glue slopping into his glove, it damn well felt like it. No way he was gonna take this ass-fuck forever. Every asshole on the line said he would just be working temporary, but here was one man gonna do something for real.

Reserving most of his anger for the company and union, Zeke jokingly vented some of it on Chicken Salad. Every ten seconds Chicken Salad mumbled in his ear, and every fifteen minutes Zeke couldn't take it anymore. He shouted over the clamor, never satisfied until he got a new reply.

"Shut up, Chicken!"

"Sumabitch."

"Someday I'm gonna glue-and-rubber your mouth."

"Sumabitch."

"I'm warning you, Chicken Sal," he shouted, shaking his glue brush under Chicken Salad's nose. "Shut up, you sumabitching old fart!"

"Holy shit!" Chicken Salad jerked back, shouting in wide-eyed surprise. "Did the lift hit yah? I'm sorry, Zeke. What happened?"

"Now you talkin'." Zeke returned to his windshields with a satisfied smile, muttering, "Now the fart be talking like a human person."

"Sumabitch."

Dogshit Miller suddenly spotted Chicken Salad staring blankly at Zeke.

"What the hell you doing, Chicken Salad?"

"Sumabitch, I didn't do nothing."

"Is that what you're paid for, O'Neill?"

"No."

"Well, get your rear in gear!"

"Yessir . . . sumabitch . . ."

Dogshit Miller moved down the line, barking, "Move it, Zeke. . . . Keep her rolling, Barney."

Zeke watched Dogshit out of the corner of his eye. The workers never answered unless the muthafucker stopped. If you were lucky, he didn't. But if he did, you could never say, "I'm sick, I can't do it." You always had to act like a little kid and say, "Well, I'm trying as hard as I can." Only other way was to start shouting and make a big scene, but most suckers didn't have the guts for it, nor the brains to keep from getting legally fired. Even if you pulled a scene, you just kissed Dogshit's ass and went back to work same as before. Hell, lately you could go back even if you pulled a pistol, as long as you kissed ass and cried like a baby. Fuckers thought they had it nailed down: kiss ass or kiss

15

off. Well, they were gonna get a showdown. He'd already filed the complaints. Most suckers didn't dare, cuz you went on the company shit list. Dogshit was already riding his ass, checking for mistakes, checking if he was working every minute. No way he'd take this shit much longer. No way he'd be a twisted pretzel like Chicken Salad.

Ronny Jenkins, a middle-aged worker with a beer belly, kicked the Coke machine several times. "Goddamn machine!" Then he dashed back to his place before Dogshit saw that he'd left the line.

Jerry Bartowski and Smokey James stood in the pits like soldiers in a trench, reaching up to spotweld the frames passing overhead. The shower of yellow-blue sparks cascaded around them, singeing their clothes, flecking their arms with flash weld burns.

The lottery man stopped his yellow forklift and knelt down beside then, rapping on Smokey's welding mask.

"Are you in this week, Smoke?"

Smokey lifted his helmet and motioned for Jerry to double-time for him. Nodding, Jerry began welding both sides of the overhead frame, his expert hands moving the sparkling iron with dazzling agility. Smokey handed the lottery man two dollars, glaring as if to say, "Why ain't I ever won this sucker? Better not be rigged, honky."

"You want two, Smoke?"

"One for Jerry. What's the payoff?"

"Good week. Three hunnerd."

As the man drove away, Smokey pocketed the tickets and, returning the favor, double-timed for Jerry.

Flipping up his helmet, Jerry reached in his

pockets which were a portable medicine chest. He went through the procedure every twenty minutes. First he took out his bottle of antihistamine and sprayed both nostrils three times, then he took out his eyedrop bottle and cleaned both eyeballs twice. Smokey thought he was Looney Tunes, but borrowed them at the end of the day.

Jerry was adjusting his earplugs, when Dogshit Miller squatted down beside him.

"This is *comp*-any time, Bartowski! Pick your ears on your *own* time!"

Blow it out your ass, Jerry thought. But he said nothing. Instead, he shot off a blinding spark shower that sent Dogshit scurrying away, and then went back to his welding.

"I'm getting brain cancer," he muttered to himself. The line was a goddamn killer. Your days were numbered even without an accident. Sure, automation was the enemy, not because it took away work but because it gave you twice as much by speeding up the line. Sure, the company speeded it up even more in violation of the pace agreement. But what the hell could you do? If you signed a grievance complaint, the company really busted your ass. If you slowed down, it just made more work for the next guy. If you really slowed down, they all jumped on your ass. Besides, on any given day, your body could do it. You could do what they wanted. It was just that it took ten years off your life, and you couldn't do shit when you got home. And if you had any tendency toward a hernia or deafness or whatever, you damn sure got all of it. Brain cancer, that would explain why he did it. The line was giving him goddamn brain cancer.

Glancing around, Ronny Jenkins motioned for

his partner to double-time for him and dashed back to the Coke machine. His throat was so hot he felt he was choking to death. He dropped in his quarter and pushed the button, but nothing happened. He jammed down the coin return, wiggled it, then furiously banged the whole machine.

"Goddamn machine! The fif-teenth time you've cheated me, you asshole bastard!"

Shaking with anger, he was ready to slam the machine onto the floor, when he spotted Dogshit Miller approaching. His face still livid, Jenkins headed back toward the line, too angry to make excuses.

"The fifteenth time," he snapped, pointing at the machine. "When you gonna get it fixed?"

"Back on the line, Jenkins."

"When you getting it fixed, Miller?"

"Tell your union rep."

3

The union hall, seedy and cramped, had cement-block walls painted the same sickly pale green as hospitals and schools. The walls were hung with grimy photo blow-ups of glories forgotten forever: solidarity meetings, laughing strikers, Presidential visits.

Nobody cared anymore. The union even paid its rank-and-file members for their attendance. Each man got three dollars for sitting through a meeting sober and awake.

The exhausted workers slouched in the folding metal chairs, the blacks and whites in separate clusters. Some were snoozing. Most sipped beer and whiskey from bottles in brown paper bags. Zeke, Jerry, and Smokey sat together on the side, sharing an unconcealed pint of Jim Beam.

"Now, the next item on tonight's agenda, and I'll keep it short."

Clarence Hill, the union representative, spoke from the podium. Forty-one, stubby and loud, he'd climbed the social ladder from greaseball blue-collar to spiffy white-collar. He now dressed with real class. He was wearing a white plastic belt, a purple silk tie, and a maroon silk shirt dotted with flapping purple swans.

"Hey, Clarence," hollered Jenkins, standing up in grease-stained clothes, his speech slurred by a pint of throat medicine.

"What is it, Ron?"

"The Coke machine! It's fifteen times the bastard's cheated me—fifteen! When you gonna make 'em fix it?"

"We'll get to you soon, Ronny. You know the Complaint Committee can't open till we finish the agenda."

"No, can't wait for the gender," Jenkins drunkenly insisted. "You gotta do it now, or I'll fall asleep and forget."

The bored crowd chuckled slightly, and Clarence played on it. "I'll wake you up, Ronny, and that's a promise. Now have a seat and drink another Coke—or whatever. We'll get to your machine."

"Damn right."

"We all know how important your Coke is to you."

Another chuckle went through the crowd. Jenkins plunked back in his chair, bumping into Chicken Salad.

"Sumabitch."

20

Clarence handled the crowd in the smooth manner of a salesman and politician, alternately regarding his former fellow workers as animals to be controlled and voters to be tricked. Shit, getting any response from these jerk-offs was hard enough, but controlling them took a real pro. After seven years he was damn good at it and, by God, he'd come up in the world. He had a big house, big car, big wardrobe. Shit, he dressed better than a goddamn lawyer. Except for the jerk-off elections, he was damn near the same as those educated guys with a guaranteed salary. The secret was to dominate these bastards and make them like it. Give them the individual treatment. Pamper some, scold others. Troublemakers like Zeke Brown were the only serious shit. But he'd come too far, by God, to let these bohunk greasers pull him down now.

He held up a leaflet, reading: "Vote *YES* on Prop. 4."

"Okay," he said, "we need two volunteers from each plant to help pass out these leaflets Saturday. We all know how important this ballot measure is. Now, who wants to help?"

The groan from the crowd was unanimous.

Clarence nodded understandingly, then gestured as if pleading for common sense.

"Now come on, boys. Nobody said it was gonna be fun? Did I say it'd be fun? Somebody's gotta do it, and if we don't do it ourselves, we'll have to use our money to hire somebody else."

Someone called out: "Whataya mean, *we*? You gonna be there, Clarence?"

The crowd snickered.

Jerry passed the pint to Smokey, muttering,

"Hell, I got two jobs already, and this bastard thinks I'm gonna hand out his asshole pamphlets on my day off."

Smokey shrugged and took a drink. He never understood why Jerry let it bother him. Fuck it, they were getting paid to sit and drink.

Jerry studied Clarence with jealous anger. Cocky bastard thought he was hot shit, strutting like a banty rooster in his goddamn red shirt, acting like those profession guys like dentists and shit. Bastard was too scared to do anything for the workers. Hell, after sitting on his fat ass for sixteen grand, the bastard was scared shitless of doing anything that might put him back on the line for nine grand a year. Bastard acted like a nun in a whorehouse, but was the biggest ass-kisser in the room. Never did nothing but screw the workers and kiss Bald Eddie's ass.

"Okay," Clarence said, "I know you're all good union boys. The union does right by you, and you do right by the union. You're doing this for yourselves—so let's have some volunteers."

Nobody stood up. Most looked at their feet. Some took a swig from their bottles.

Zeke fumed in his chair, forcing his anger to pump up his confidence. Find a way, dammit. Fuckers were all the same. Union bosses, company big shots, they had more toilets in their house than the plant had on the line. The way these union fuckheads talked, you'd think there was no line at all. Fuckers had a nice position on ballots, a nice position on civil rights, a nice position on everything but the muthafucking conditions kicking ass outa guys on the line. Fuckers thought workers were shit, and black workers worse than shit. The

22

brothers always be the last hired and first fired, and never be getting the skilled jobs. Let the workers eat shit, let the niggers eat the leftovers. Well, this nigger was gonna dump a truckload of shit. He'd stick Clarence with the locker again, then find a way to put a real hurting on his ass. Bring the fucker down, in front of everybody. Just find a way, dammit.

Zeke stood up, raising his hand.

"Zeke," said Clarence, "I knew we could count on you. Who's gonna be next?"

"No," Zeke said, "I'm busy Saturday. I wanna talk about the union doing right by me—like you said."

Clarence sighed loudly with exasperation, encouraging the crowd to join him.

"What is it now, Zeke?"

"My locker door. The handle's been broke for six months now and the company still ain't fixed it. The only way I can open it is to stick my little finger in the hole. I cut my finger and that was two weeks ago and it still ain't healed yet. So now I gotta use ball-point pens, which keep breaking."

The workers groaned, having heard about the damn locker for five months. Clarence gave them a nod of approval.

"Be reasonable, Zeke."

"Reasonable! I been waiting six months, Clarence, and you ain't done shit! You call that reasonable? You're my rep. You're supposed to take this to the Green Room and get it settled."

"Now, Zeke." Clarence motioned for Zeke to calm down, then aimed his hard-facts-of-life routine at the crowd. "You know I can't take every little thing to the Green Room. I gotta wait for something big, or a bunch of little things. By God, we can't let our power be dissipated by the plant."

"Plant! The brothers've heard this bullshit before, Jack. You know what *plant* is? Plant is just short for *plan*-tation!"

A young black worker shouted: "Right on, brother!"

Several white workers raised their eyes to the ceiling for help. Was he gonna start this rap again?

Someone groaned, "Sit down, man."

"Lemme have my three bucks, will ya?"

"Okay, okay," droned Clarence, quickly restoring order. This racial shit could blow your ass off. You had to be careful but firm. "Okay, now that Zeke's finished, let's—"

"I'll catch them dice, Jack!" Zeke shouted Clarence down, too angry to be stopped by anything. "I'm gonna take my case to the head man himself! I'm going straight to union headquarters, then I'll get some fair rep-re-sen-ta-tion!"

The crowd, sparked by his energy, began muttering their approval.

"That of course is your right," said Clarence calmly, frowning as the situation threatened to get out of hand.

"Not only that, Jack!" Zeke felt himself shift into high gear and began playing to the crowd. "I'm gonna run for union rep myself! I'm gonna win your job and give the brothers some real representation!"

The mutters of approval grew unanimous.

Clarence backed away from the podium. Shit, give the crazy bastard enough rope and he'd hang his own ass.

24

Zeke saw the crowd was waiting for him, but they could still go either way. His wiry body twitched with tension, his motor running so fast he had no idea what he'd say next.

"Real representation, Jack! Gonna make some *real* changes around here! And then—and then maybe I'll just fly out to Palm Springs and drop in on Bald Eddie's new vacation house, and maybe hit a few golf balls with Frank Fitzsimmons and Mr. Nixon."

The crowd burst into raucous cheers. Both the blacks and whites yelled out their approval.

"Tell it like it is, brother!"

"You tell 'em, Zeke!"

Zeke gestured as if swinging a golf club. "Those union big shots. I always wanted to see how those guys live. You know what I mean?"

"Say it, brother!"

"I heard something," he said, directing their attention at Clarence with his golf swing. "Maybe Clarence would know. I heard those guys got more pisspots in their house than the plant's got on the whole goddamn line."

The room exploded with hoots of laughter, the workers slapping each other's palms in agreement.

Zeke beamed with satisfaction. Damn, but he'd finally done it. He'd turned the whole local against Clarence's ass. Someday he'd glue-and-rubber the racist muthafucker to the wall.

Clarence crossed his arms and glared at Zeke. By God, he'd nail that jerk-off nigger. Just find the right time. Like Bald Eddie said, "Never get in a slop-eating contest with pigs or a shit-eating contest with niggers."

25

The usual Happy Hour crowd was back at Oogie's by seven-thirty. Zeke, Jerry, and Smokey sat at their usual table, joking together while drinking up Clarence's "easy three" dollars. Zeke, in a wild quicksilver mood, was accepting free drinks from admirers and bubbling with kick-ass energy.

One admirer was the new kid on the line, Bobby Joe McGraw, a Southern boy of nineteen with a long blond ponytail. Asking their permission, he'd bought a round of Stroh's and joined the table, his hard hat resting beside his elbow.

Zeke had no time to listen to praise. He was too delighted with this chance to zing the new boy. Winking at Jerry, he was soon telling Bobby Joe about the first time Smokey got sent to the state penitentiary in Jackson. He spoke in hushed tones, as if having Smokey overhear him was dangerous. He began by giving elaborate bullshit-descriptions of all the horrendous crimes Smokey didn't get sent up for, bewildering Bobby Joe with his sly attempts to hook Smokey into telling the real story. But Smokey refused to bite.

Bobby Joe finally whispered to Zeke: "Well, what *did* he do?"

"Nothing," said Smokey.

"Come on, Smoke," Zeke urged openly. "The boy gotta learn sometime. Tell him how it's done."

"Wasn't nothin'."

"Big talker, ain't he? Shit, I'll tell you myself. Smokey was a heavy mutha at Jackson, cuz he got busted for—"

Zeke stopped abruptly, his quick eyes focused across the room where Hank, a lanky white worker in a cowboy shirt, was dropping a quarter in the jukebox. He called out: "Hey, Hank! Don't be

26

playing none of those goddamn cowboy songs."

"No way, Zeke." Hank laughed good-naturedly. "This is *my* money. Get some from your welfare lady."

"Be cool, white brother," Zeke shouted calmly, then muttered to himself. "Muthafucking cowboy." He sipped his beer and eagerly returned to Bobby Joe: "Anyway, this goes back a few years when Smokey was still learning about the pussy. He was visiting the wife of a friend, who was outa town. Now this bitch be a good teacher, but ugly. I mean, ug-lyyy!"

"Not *that* ugly," Smokey muttered.

"Anyway, ol' Smokey's in there, humping and pumping cuz this nympho bitch can't get enough. I mean, the bitch'll fuck anything—dogs, chickens, squirrels . . ."

"Wait a minute, nigger," Smokey said, pissed off that Zeke was hooking him. "Shit, wasn't that way at all. I was there with my friend Leroy cuz this lady likes fucking two guys at a time. She says everything's cool cuz her old man be long gone. Outa town, she said."

Smokey suddenly stopped.

Bobby Joe said, "And?"

Smokey gave Zeke an exasperated glance, then continued reluctantly. "So just when we get to really smoking, I hear her old man come stomping up the stairs. Now I know this crazy fucker. George Washington Coleman. Know his step. Cra-zy fucker. Always got a gun. He don't care, he shoots your ass."

Smokey stopped again. Fuck it, he wasn't going on, no matter what Zeke did.

Zeke took over, saying whatever popped into his

head and making exaggerated gestures. "So George Washington Coleman be pounding on the door and the bitch be screaming, 'George is back, what'll we do?' And Smokey be looking out the fifth-floor window, praying, 'Oh God, just for one minute let these arms become wings!' "

"Shit, wasn't like that at all," said Smokey, waiting for them to stop laughing. "Leroy and me knew there was only one way out and that was to go *over* him. So on a signal Leroy opens the door and I hit the dude in the balls and mouth, and the sucker drops like a stone. Except the sucker wasn't George Washington at all, but the police. Goddamn cop trying to ask about somebody next door."

Bobby Joe said, "So?"

"So we cut out, but there was two more pigs waiting with cuffs and sticks."

"Why didn't you just explain?"

"Listen, boy. Nigger hit a roller on Twelfth Street, he don't stick around to explain."

"Jesus, you mean you got three years for hitting a cop?"

"No," Zeke said. "He got the trey the next time around, and that was even dumber. He blew the cat away."

"Yeah," said Jerry, "it was a friend."

"Wasn't my fault," said Smokey. "Those crazy wife-bitches do anything to get fucked."

Bobby Joe gave him a puzzled look. "You mean your wife don't mind?"

"Shit," Smokey muttered, looking away.

Zeke leaned forward confidentially: "Ol' Smokey don't need no wife."

"Why's that?"

"Cuz he's got yours."

Jerry and Zeke rocked back with laughter, Jerry almost falling off his chair. Even Smokey was laughing. Bobby Joe just stared at them, his mouth open like he'd been hit on the jaw.

Jerry leaned over to him: "Watch out for that big nigger, he'll get your wife's pussy stretched way outa shape."

Zeke laughed so hard he choked on his beer, but managed to sputter: "Better than Polack dick. Polack wife lay back, screaming, 'Is it in yet?' "

"Shit," Jerry said, standing up to leave. "Least I work for my family, spearchucker. Time for me to pump some gas."

"Yeah," said Zeke, "I gotta split too."

Smokey nodded and said, "I'm having a party Saturday night. With some of my 'friends,' you know?"

"Now you talking, my man. When?"

"Midnight."

"We'll see you then."

Zeke and Jerry walked out the door together. The room was suddenly quiet. Several men approached the jukebox. Smokey stared at the door, then looked at Bobby Joe.

"Time for you to buy more beer, boy."

4

The living-room furnishings were shabby discount-store merchandise. Carolyn tried not to be embarrassed. She prided herself on keeping the house clean and in good repair. But she couldn't help wincing when her friends saw the frayed sofa, the mended lampshades, the carpet with a well-worn path from the front door to the dining room. Whenever she asked for something new, Zeke always refused. He was still making the payments on the old stuff. Their only recent purchase was the large console TV, dominating the end of the room.

Zeke slouched in his easy chair and watched *The Jeffersons,* his least favorite program. He never just listened to it. He always talked back. As the well-dressed black man fluttered around the lavishly furnished living room, Zeke spouted an endless stream of epithets.

"Goddamn skinny Oreo . . . How'd a dumb nigger like that get so much money? Sold his ass . . . Little shrimp, with all his goddamn honky friends . . ."

Carolyn, watching from the sofa, tried to ignore his familiar bitching. She saw the playful spark of romance in his eye tonight. Behind the incessant gripes, he was actually in a high-flying mood. But finally she couldn't hear the program at all.

"If you hate it so much, why don't you turn it off?"

"Say what?"

"Turn it off."

"Woman!" He pointed his bottle at the TV, spilling beer on the carpet. "I worked three years for that sucker, and I'm damn well gonna watch it. Only thing that works in this house anyway."

"Okay, honey."

She had her reasons for letting it ride. For one thing, he was right about the landlord never doing anything but collect. If he hadn't paid for and done it himself, the plumbing would still be leaking through the ceiling. If only he could find time and money to fix the heating before winter and the hawk almost froze the kids to death in their beds again. For another thing, he took a lotta crap at work but never took it out on his family, like lotsa guys did. Betty Van Stee across the street was bedridden twice a month from Hank's beatings. Once the Van Stee kids even came knocking on the door in the middle of the night, begging to stay over cuz Hank was busting everything with a baseball bat. The most Zeke ever did was gripe, groan, and growl.

"Rich shrimp . . . Never worked a day in his life . . ."

Liston, Ali, and Dennis suddenly began scrapping. The three boys were playing "The Game of Jaws" on the floor.

"You lost," said Liston, grabbing the plastic shark. "It's my turn."

"Dennis pushed my arm," said Ali.

"Bullshit, I didn't touch you."

Ali, trying to grab back the shark, broke the plastic jaw. They all glanced up at Zeke.

"You in trouble now," said Liston. "Daddy gonna kung-fu your ass."

Zeke leaned down to fix the toy. "What the shit. Can't you boys take turns? You can count, can't you?"

They all mumbled yes.

"Shit," Zeke muttered, seeing the damage was beyond repair. "This junk's as bad as the cars we make. Next time I'll be buying those un-break-a-ble toys. Like maybe wood blocks."

"It wasn't no good anyway," muttered Ali.

Zeke handed him the toy. "Maybe you can figger out how to *pay* for it, smart ass. Maybe you can become a rich Uncle Tom and get on the TV with lotsa rich white friends."

"Son of a bitch," whined Dennis. "They broke it. Not me."

"Don't say that," Zeke threatened. "Never say that word, Dennis. I hear that sumabitchin' Chicken Salad say it a million times a day."

"Bull," challenged Ali. "Nobody says a million words a day."

32

"Get your pencil, smart ass."

"Why?"

"Since you wanna play the numbers, you can play with *these* numbers—ten times a minute, eight hours a day, fifty weeks a year. Figger it out, Ali. If I hear that word less than a million times a year, I'll pay you twenty-five cents cash."

"Me too, Daddy?"

"Okay, I'll pay you each a goddamn quarter."

"Promise?"

"Yeah, and I hope you win."

The boys were busy scribbling on the coffee table when the doorbell suddenly rang. Zeke got up to answer it and Carolyn said, "If that's your brother, tell him we already ate."

Zeke flipped on the porch light and carefully opened the door a few inches. Standing on the porch was a middle-aged white man with a briefcase. Dressed in a suit, tie, and thick glasses, he spoke with a nasal voice.

"Mr. Brown? I'm John Berg from the Internal Revenue Service."

"No," Zeke said, slowly closing the door. "Don't want none, Jack. Can't afford it."

Berg stuck his shoe in the doorway. "It's about your income tax, Mr. Brown. I know this is the right address."

Zeke glanced around, searching for a way to get rid of the guy. Suddenly he whispered confidentially, "Me and my woman was just gonna, you know, make some love. Dig?"

"I can come back with a police officer if you like."

Zeke swung open the door with exaggerated friendliness. "Oh, you the tax man! Whyn't you say so? Come on in. Carolyn, get this man a beer."

"Nothing, thanks. Not while I'm working."

"Have a seat," Zeke said, eying him suspiciously and motioning for Carolyn to get a beer.

"Thank you." Berg sat on the sofa and opened his briefcase. "This'll just take a minute, Mr. Brown. I wanted to catch you at home."

"I hope there's no problem," said Zeke, sitting down and reaching for his Stroh's.

"In checking your return, we've found two discrepancies. First, you are claiming nine deductions for dependents."

"That's right. Me and Carolyn have had one each year. We call them children."

"But according to the hospital records, you only have five children—all boys."

"I can't afford no hospital for *all* my kids."

"What do you mean?"

"Look at that form. Shit, I don't take home a hundred bucks a week. Government, state, social security, union dues, credit payments, the credit man especially, they get all the rest. By the time I—"

"Excuse me, Mr. Brown. I'd just like to see your sons to make sure." Berg opened a folder and read the names. "We have Sugar Ray Brown, Ezekiel Brown Junior, Liston Brown, Ali Brown, Gayle Sayers Brown, Dennis Brown, James Brown, O.J. Simpson Brown, and Stevie Wonder Brown."

"That's right."

"I see. Who's Stevie Wonder?"

"He's a singer," said Carolyn, coming in with a beer, her look at Zeke saying, "I *told* you not to use that one."

"I see. Where are the boys now?"

34

"Here are Liston, Ali, and Dennis," said Zeke. "Sugar Ray and Zeke Junior got a ball game tonight. The rest are out on the streets. Never can keep track of those boys. Carolyn, why don't you try to go find them?"

Carolyn glanced at him quizzically, then left with the boys.

Berg opened another folder. "The other thing, Mr. Brown. Our records show you held a part-time job last year and didn't declare it."

"Sure you won't have a beer?"

"Not while I'm working. You worked twenty days as a house painter."

"Somebody musta made a mistake," said Zeke, growing quieter as he got angrier.

"The mistake appears to be yours. I'm sure it's just an oversight on your part, but you'll have to pay the back taxes nonetheless. Plus the late penalty, of course."

Carolyn had taken her sons to the house next door. Mary, her neighbor, was overweight and warmhearted. She called her two boys into the kitchen and said, "Here's Junior and Billy. You can use them."

"I need two more," said Carolyn. "Zeke got beside himself this year and claimed we had nine kids."

"Nine! Has the man lost his mind? Even white folks ain't gonna believe that, honey. When you supposed to start having them? In the first grade?"

"I guess so," Carolyn smiled. "When's Fred get home?"

"After midnight. How about Carla's boys?"

"No, too old. Besides, you know how Carla is."

"Yeah, too bad them Van Stee boys is white,"

35

Mary laughed. "They the right age, but white as lepers. Maybe use blackface."

"Yes," Carolyn said seriously.

"Huh? Don't you go losing your mind too, honey."

"No, I was thinking. If you've got some extra clothes, my boys could switch."

"Worth a try."

"Okay," Carolyn said, kneeling down beside Dennis. "Take off your clothes, boys. Dennis, remember you're James. Ali, you're O.J."

"That's easy, Mama. Cuz I really am O.J."

Zeke slouched deeper in his chair and watched Berg push the little buttons on the pocket calculator. Whatever the goddamn figure was, he didn't have ten dollars to his name. He'd emptied the bank account having Liston's tonsils taken out, and the goddamn heating was still busted, and now the tax man. It was gonna be a cold winter.

"Here we are," Berg said. "It's only two hundred ninety dollars for the second job, but when you add that to the three false deductions over a period of six years, it comes out to two thousand four hundred sixty dollars and seventy-five cents."

"You crazy? Where am I gonna get that kinda money?"

Carolyn entered the room with Junior and Billy. Liston, Ali, and Dennis followed in oversized clothes. Zeke sprung to his feet, enormously relieved.

"Gayle, James, where you been? Damn, can never find those boys. Come on in. Don't be shy."

Berg got to his feet. He wasn't fooled for a minute. "Very impressive, Mrs. Brown. This is gonna take longer than I planned. Let's get all the boys together and go through the records. I'll wait for the others if necessary."

Zeke, seeing the game was up, let his real anger flash out. "What was that number, mutha? Two-four-six-oh? All right, get outa here!"

Berg was irritated. "Look, Mr. Brown, I'm trying to do you a favor by coming here. It's not my fault if you can't support your family. You make a hundred ninety dollars a week and if you can't—"

"Get out!"

"Mr. Brown, there's no reason to—"

"Get out, muthafucker!"

Berg turned pale and reached for his briefcase. "It's not me, Mr. Brown. We all work for the government. I'm just—"

"Git, mutha!" Carolyn tried to stop him, but Zeke stuck his fist in front of Berg's eyes. "You've done your slumming for tonight! Now git your ass outa here before I stick my fist up it!"

Berg edged toward the front door, clutching his briefcase and snapping, "You'll pay, Mr. Brown. You'll still—"

"You'll get my money! Now get outa my house! I gotta live here, you piece of shit!"

Berg hurried through the doorway into the night.

"Goddamn asshole! I don't hafta take this shit! I'd talk big too if the Army supported me with all their bombs and shit! I ain't gonna take this shit!"

Carolyn watched her husband shouting his rage at the dark empty street, his eyes burning with hatred, his romantic sparkle completely gone. She rubbed his shoulders to calm him down. He threw his arm around her and stumbled back into the house, still trembling with rage.

Jerry stood under the gas station's blue fluorescent lights, wearing his blue Bardahl racing jacket in the cool night air. He pulled the nozzle out of the car and hung it on the rusty pump, then approached the car. The driver was John Burrows, the phony professor and F.B.I. agent. Jerry just stared at him, saying nothing.

"How much?"

"Three bucks."

Burrows took a long time finding the money. "Had a good time the other day. I liked your friends. There was something I wanted to ask you."

"I don't know nothin'."

"I was gonna drop by your house and see if—"

"Listen, turkey, *nobody* comes near my house. Nobody I don't invite."

"You know Clarence Hill, don't you? You used to be his key man before he got promoted to union rep. I hear he just bought a house in Woodland Hills."

"I don't know nothing about that."

"Come on," Burrows said, paying the three dollars.

"Don't know nothing about no house, nothing about no Clarence, nothing about no union. I don't know shit."

"Everybody knows your local's the most corrupt in the city."

"Yeah? Well, I'll tell you what I know. I know you got your man inside the union, and the union's got its man inside the government. And if I farted upwind, I'd be out of a job in an hour."

"But you don't think I'd—"

"I don't think nothin'," said Jerry, getting angry. "Just leave me alone, turkey. I don't talk to no government agent. I don't talk to no rollers of any kind."

Jerry tapped the car fender and walked into the station. Punching the cash register, he noticed Burrows still watching him from the car. Damn, these bastards track your ass like a goddamn bird dog.

5

Saturday morning Zeke drove his Chevy station wagon into downtown Detroit and parked across the street from union headquarters. One way to get off the line was to get in with Bald Eddie. He crossed the street and walked inside.

The office was strictly business and nothing fancy. The walls were dirty, the windows smudged, the linoleum cracked. Several men were huddled around a table, packing leaflets which said "Vote YES on Prop. 4."

Zeke glanced around. The desks and filing cabinets were made of scratched sheet metal. But the huge walk-in safe was forged steel with a combination lock of shiny brass. The thick door stood open. A red-haired secretary walked out with a small metal box.

The security guard sat in the corner, gazing out the window and picking his nose. When he saw Zeke watching him, he quickly pulled out his finger and wiped it on his pants.

Zeke approached Janet, the attractive young black secretary at the main desk.

"My name is Ezekiel Brown. I'm here to see Mr. Johnson."

"Just a minute," she said, not looking up as she finished writing a note.

"Hey," said Zeke, flashing on the charm. "How come they got you working on Saturday, girl?"

"Working on Proposition Four."

"I was thinking of a different proposition. When you gonna have time to hit the town?"

Looking up, she said, "I don't even know you, Mr. Brown."

"We can fix that fast."

"Frankly, I don't want to."

"Whew! You be *cold*, girl. You locked up tighter than that safe."

Ignoring him, Janet punched the intercom and said, "Mr. Johnson, Mr. Ezekiel Brown is here."

The intercom said, "Send him in."

Janet pointed to the unmarked door in back. Zeke took a deep breath to build up his confidence, then turned the doorknob and walked inside.

Bald Eddie Johnson, fifty-five, overweight, had the confident look of a man accustomed to power for a long time. He projected equal amounts of glad-hand friendliness and hard-ass toughness.

His office decor was calculated to convey a sense of personal authority while dispelling any rumors of personal wealth. Nothing was plush. He tried to look like one of the guys. But the walls were

41

hung with framed photos of himself with people like President Kennedy and Jimmy Hoffa.

Bald Eddie leaned across his desk and gave Zeke a soul-brother handshake. He did it awkwardly but with a big smile. It took Zeke completely by surprise and he responded with equal awkwardness. As they fumbled with each other's hands, Zeke stared at the smiling face, wondering what the guy was trying to prove. Damn, these power big shots were stone weird.

"Glad to meet you, Zeke. Have a seat."

"Thanks."

"What's the problem?"

"I want to complain about Clarence Hill, Mr. Johnson. He—"

"Call me Bald Eddie."

Zeke nodded. Fucker didn't care shit about the union. Only number in his book was Number One. You couldn't even touch his throne without having something to make the big shot even bigger. Gotta find something he needs, but first you gotta leave your calling card. Give him some shit to remember you by.

"Something about Clarence, Zeke?"

"Yeah, he's our rep, the shop steward at the Dearborn plant. How'd he get his job?"

"What do you mean?"

"The man is a racist."

"How's that?"

"He's a racist," Zeke repeated, hardly knowing what he'd say next. "He ain't looking out for the black men at all. The white brothers get everything fixed right away. But the bloods don't get shit. When my Daddy come up from Alabama, all he could say was: 'Where do I go to make them cars?' My brother, my uncles, my cousins—we been making Fords and Chevys all our lives. And what we got to show for it?"

"Zeke," Bald Eddie said firmly. "You know of course that our locals were the first to insist on black-white parity. We have the best black-white relations in the union."

"Don't get me wrong. The union's done right by blacks on wages. But wages ain't the problem no more."

"What is?"

"The whole thing," Zeke said. He had a million things to say, but his anger was too big for words. Hell, the problem was everywhere, pounding on your ass every day. "It's the racism, and the line conditions—and these goddamn prices. Everything keeps going up. The more we make, the less it's worth."

"Zeke," Bald Eddie said impatiently. "What exactly is the problem?"

"My locker. It ain't been fixed for six months now and Clarence won't do nothin'. Two weeks ago I cut my—"

Bald Eddie grabbed the phone. "Janet, get me Clarence Hill. He'll be at home." Looking up, he said, "How long you been on the line, Zeke?"

"Seven years. A year at Buick's and two at Chrysler's."

Bald Eddie heard Janet's voice on the phone: "Mr. Hill must be out. There's no answer."

Realizing Zeke hadn't heard her, Bald Eddie pushed a button for another line and pretended to talk with Hill. "Hello, Clarence. . . . I'm fine. I'm

43

here with Zeke Brown. He's having some trouble with his locker. See that it gets fixed. . . . Fine, Clarence, keep me informed. Talk to you later."

Smiling, Bald Eddie hung up the dead phone and said, "That oughta take care of it, Zeke. Is there anything else?"

"No, not right now." Zeke moved toward the door, impressed with Bald Eddie's ability to get fast action. Fucker was Looney Tunes but he sure was the main man. "Thanks a lot, Mr. Johnson. This is a real load off my mind."

"Call me Bald Eddie."

"Yeah. Thanks, Bald Eddie."

"Anytime, Zeke."

Zeke returned to the outer office, feeling satisfied with himself. Janet was on the phone. The security guard was reading a girlie magazine. The red-haired secretary wheeled a bicycle out of the safe and headed for the front door.

Zeke opened the door for her, but kept staring at the open safe. Shit, that's where all them union dues be. Sucker was loaded. With money like that, a man could change his address. No more living on 22 Boogie Woogie Avenue, thirteen garbage cans to the left.

Jerry and Arlene were in bed before midnight, getting ready to sleep. Jerry tossed restlessly for a while, then suddenly looked at the alarm clock and said, "Oh, damn!"

"Damn what?"

"Pumps," he said, getting up. "I forgot to lock one of the pumps."

"Do you have to do it *now*? Do it in the morning?"

44

"Can't," he said, pulling on his jeans. "You want me to pay for all the gas stolen tonight? Besides, honey, in the morning I wanna sleep in with you."

Watching him, Arlene had a pretty good idea of what was going on. "Will you go to Mass with us in the morning? The kids should see their father in church, Jerry."

"Okay," he sighed. "Just this once." Hell, why did the good shit always have a penalty? At least she didn't know, or did she?

Zeke was getting dressed at the same time. Carolyn watched him from the bed. He had a new routine, but she knew exactly what was going down.

"I told you this morning," he said, pulling on his pants. "I gotta help Freddy move into his new apartment. If he don't move at night, he's gotta pay his back rent."

"If you're gonna be working, how come you're putting on your new pants?"

"New! You call these new? These ain't new."

"They sure ain't old."

"What you want, woman? You want me walking around like some criminal? Is that what you want?"

"What shirt you gonna wear?"

"Just this old rag over here," he said, reaching for a grease-stained workshirt.

"I know what you're doing," she said. "Don't think you're fooling me, nigger."

Twenty minutes later Jerry parked his battered old Ford under the dim streetlight in front of Smokey's drab apartment building. Zeke's station wagon was parked across the street. Zeke tossed his grease-stained work shirt in the back and slipped on a floral rayon party shirt.

Laughing, Jerry approached him and said, "Hey, how'd you get away from your old lady?"

"Shit, sucker, *my* woman knows her place."

"Hell, you probably got her handcuffed to the bed."

"Handcuffs! Who's got money for handcuffs? I use the clothesline."

Laughing together, they entered the building, knocked on the door, and when it opened slapped Smokey's palm.

"Hey, brother," Zeke said. "What's happening?"

"Hey, blood," Smokey mumbled, already flying high. He seemed almost relaxed. His face had lost its sullen ready-to-punch-out-the-world look.

He motioned them inside his passion pit with a big smile. The funky fluff furnishings were blood red. The thick red carpet resembled an enormous bed strewn with red pillows and silver cushions. The silver walls were hung with "black light" paintings of voluptuous nude black women.

Four half-nude young women sat around the coffee table. Cathy and Flo were black, Bobbie and Sugar white. Using rolled-up dollar bills, they were sniffing thin rows of cocaine.

Zeke rushed forward and said, "Cat, my girl, you looking fine."

"Ca-*thy* to you," Cathy said. "You looking older."

Ignoring the insult, Zeke knelt beside her. "Slip aside and let me have some of that nose candy."

"Jesus," said Jerry, gazing at all the white gold. "There must be three weeks' pay here, Smoke."

Smokey grinned and held up his fingers. "Four weeks, brother."

Zeke finished a hit and said, "Smokey's a real family man just like us. Spend all his pay on his family

—and all the family he's got is you and me and these beautiful girls here."

"Shit," Cathy said. "Is jive-talking all you can do, nigger?"

"Say what, bitch? Don't worry about me? I'll do you until the sparks fly off your pussy."

"Shit," she laughed, "I'd sure like to see that."

"You just worry about Jerry here. These white folks don't know nothin' about the fucking. He thinks his wife got pregnant on the telephone."

"Hell," Jerry laughed, unzipping his jeans. "At least it was my telephone. In fact, I think I'm getting a long-distance call right now."

"Yeah," Zeke laughed, "probably from the Alaska pipeline."

Soon everyone was undressed and the stereo was moaning Marvin Gaye's "You Sure Love to Ball." Everything became a swirling haze of coke and booze and grass, a series of slow-flowing pleasures with short spells of clear-eyed jokes and shouts.

An hour later Zeke was sprawled on the floor, fucked out for the moment, sipping a bottle of Wild Turkey and trying to talk. But nobody was listening. Smokey was busy going at it with Cathy and Bobbie in one corner, while Jerry and Flo did the same in another.

"Smoke," Zeke shouted, "listen to me! You shoulda see that sucker, man. Biggest I ever seen in my whole life. Mutha's so big you could walk in standing up. Damn, Jerry! You hear me?"

Jerry, busy with Flo, looked across the room at Smokey and shouted, "Who's he talking about?"

"Shit if I know," said Smokey, shrugging without breaking his motion.

Zeke staggered to his feet, shouting, "*What*, not

who, suckers! The safe at union headquarters. Mutha's so big one bitch keeps her bicycle in it."

Sugar stepped out of the bathroom and approached him. "Think you can get it up again, Zeke?"

"Shit," Zeke muttered, bleary-eyed, dropping his whiskey bottle. "Come here, girl. Can ol' Zeke get it up again? Is Martin Luther King in heaven?"

Three hours later Zeke and Smokey walked out of the bedroom with Flo and Sugar. Zeke was talking again.

"I didn't say we should, just that it was a knock-over. You shoulda seen the mutha. Must have a truckload of money."

Entering the living room, they saw Jerry going down on Cathy on the sofa. Smokey went to the coffee table for more cocaine. Zeke wobbled over to Jerry and slapped his bare ass, saying, "You hear me, sucker?"

"Mmm."

"Enough money for all of us." Zeke waited a moment for him to respond, then tickled Jerry's foot. "I'm talking to you, Jerry."

Jerry peered over Cathy's thigh, wiped his lips and squinted at Zeke with bleary-eyed irritation. "Uh, I'm a little preoccupied, you know?"

"Well, who ain't, sucker? Preoccupied! Shit, what you mean pre-oc-cu-pied? What you think this is —postwar Germany?"

"Shit," Cathy said. "Can't you see he's busy? Ain't often a woman gets a *real* man."

"That's just cuz no *black* man would eat no pussy. Shit, he's just making reparations."

By dawn the women were gone and the smoke-filled room was quiet. Zeke, Jerry, and Smokey slouched side by side on the sofa. Gray light filtered bleakly through the curtain behind them. They shared a quart of Wild Turkey to stay free and a quart of skim milk to get sober. Each man spoke almost to himself, looking for a good reason to stand up and go back to the real world, to face the personal corner of hell awaiting his return.

"Shit," Jerry mumbled. "Every time I get coked up like this I think I'm never goin' back to the plant. Don't know why the fuck I do."

"Credit man," Smokey muttered.

"Yeah. Credit's the only thing the company gives you free. Got me a TV, fridge, dishwasher, washer-dryer, motorcycle, stereo, buy this shit, buy that shit. All you got is a bunch of shit you don't own and you can't unload cuz it's already broke down."

"Damn," Zeke said. "I gotta get three grand in ninety days or the IRS gonna start docking my paycheck for back taxes. Then I can forget about toys and clothes and shit. I won't even be able to feed my kids."

"Gas station ain't no better," said Jerry. "Goddamn two fifty an hour. I must have fucking brain cancer."

"Put in for extra overtime on the line," Smokey said.

"I hate the line."

Zeke put his hand over his eyes. "God, sometimes I get so depressed, thinking about all the things I promised to do for Carolyn. All the things I ain't done, and know I ain't never gonna do. Man's supposed to take care of his woman. Supposed to keep his kids from living in shit. Keep his family from . . ."

Zeke stopped, his throat almost clogged with

tears. Nobody said anything for a moment. Finally Zeke cleared his throat and changed the subject.

"Goddamn money. Never could hold onto it. Never got the knack of that shit. I just ain't got the knack for money. Good thing Smokey's got no family to worry about. Otherwise we'd never have a good time."

Jerry nodded. "I swore I wouldn't work during my vacation this year."

"Smoke," Zeke said, "where can I get three grand? I ain't gonna go to no dago loan shark. Those cats mess with your family."

"Hit the safe you always talking about."

"You crazy? That's our own union."

"You said it was a knockover."

"Shit," Zeke said. "That was just the coke talking."

"Is it a knockover or not?"

"It's a knockover, all right. Baby food. Just protected by some honky who be picking his nose all day. Ain't even a real roller."

"Then hit it," Smokey said, leaning forward.

"Our own union?"

"Fuck, they ain't done shit for us."

Jerry sat up and began laughing. "Damn, that'd really be a killer, wouldn't it?"

Zeke grinned. "Yeah, we'd just be taking what was ours in the first place."

"Now you be talking, brother. How many night guards?"

"I don't know."

"Let's find out. What do you think, Jerry?"

"Nah, I couldn't."

"Somebody oughta," Zeke said. "Teach them

fuckers a lesson. They put a hurting on our ass as bad as the company."

"Ain't no way to do it," Jerry said, taking a swig of milk. "But I'd sure like to see the look on their faces."

6

The workers gathered around the lunch tables and vending machines for their first coffee break. Though the heavy machinery was silent, the clamorous pounding continued inside their heads. They hated feeling awake, especially on Mondays. Nobody wanted to know it was four days to payday again. But two hours on the line had defeated all their efforts to stay asleep.

Older workers had survival techniques to fall back on. They could go into blissful trances of nothingness, or construct elaborate two-hour sex fantasies. But the younger guys couldn't go back without sleep-walking medicine. They used mostly marijuana and tranquilizers, calculating the dosage carefully. They had to achieve a delicate balance: drugged enough to blot out the reality of the line, but alert enough to dodge the reality of fatal accidents.

Chicken Salad split a pack of Twinkies with Barney, while Hank bitched about the Detroit Tigers. Bobby Joe sat across from them, munching granola and reading his paperback *Catch-22*. Ronny Jenkins was at the poker table. Alice Kowalski sat at the corner table, watching the young guys smoke grass and knitting a sweater for her new baby.

Zeke, Jerry, and Smokey sat on a bench by the locker room, drinking from plastic cups of coffee spiked with bourbon.

"Yeah," Zeke said quietly. "Me and Smoke been thinking about it. We're gonna talk some more at Oogie's."

"The union job?"

Zeke motioned for Jerry to keep his voice down. "Yeah. You want in?"

Before Jerry could answer, Chicken Salad shouted to everyone: "Here comes Dogshit Miller already."

Dogshit strode in the room. "Come on, you donkeys! Get a move on. Line starts rolling in thirty seconds."

"We know, Miller. We know." Bobby Joe closed his book and walked beside Chicken Salad. "You been here a long time, Salad. How'd Dogshit get his job?"

"Sumabitch, I dunno."

Jerry and Smokey trudged together to their stations on the endless line. Jerry sprayed his nostrils and said, "Have you got any, uh, side effects?"

"From what?"

"The party."

"Just a hangover."

"No," Jerry said, "I mean like crotch rot."

"You crazy? Those girls are clean."

"Yeah," Jerry sighed, nodding with resignation. "That's what I figured. I've got me another case of the psychosomatic crabs."

"Shit." Smokey grinned and reached for his welding helmet. "You're fucked up, Jerry."

"Yeah," Jerry nodded, scratching himself. "And they always get me worst when I'm with Arlene."

The buzzer rang and the line began rolling. The pounding of the gigantic metal presses shook the building. Forklifts and sparking welding irons filled the air with smoke.

Overhead somewhere out of sight "mules" lowered frames onto the line. Workers power-buffed the brilliant colors of the metal parts: sunflower yellow, glacial blue, cranberry red, sandalwood, pewter, lime. Others installed steering wheels and power-bolted the seats. Doors, hoods, and trunks were power-riveted into place. Workers power-hoisted the motors into position. Others connected the wires and hoses. Then somewhere out of sight six gallons of gas were injected, the engine ignited, and another unit plopped off the line.

After another three hundred minutes and three hundred cars, punctuated by a half-hour lunch break, Ronny Jenkins motioned for his partner to double-time and dashed into the lunch room to the vending machines. He stuck his quarter in the Coke machine and, once again, nothing happened.

"Six-teen times, you bastard!"

Exploding with rage, he charged the machine with his whole overweight body and pounded it with his fists. Then he suddenly stood still, pointing his bloody fist at it with cold determined fury.

"This is the last time you're gonna fuck me, you goddamn asshole machine!"

Glancing around, he saw Alice Kowalski passing on her yellow forklift with a load of batteries. He raced over, grabbed her hand, and pulled her out of the driver's seat. She backed away from him and shouted: "Jenkins! What're you doing!"

He jumped into the seat, dumped the load of batteries on the floor, and accelerated jerkily toward the lunch room. Raising the forks to eye level, he drove the screeching forklift straight toward the Coke machine. Both forks crashed through the glass panel of cola cans and skewered the machine to the wall.

The line stopped and the workers rushed forward to watch.

Jenkins thrashed his arms and legs in a frenzy of organized rage. He lifted the forks, jammed the shift into reverse, and backed up fifteen feet from the cement wall. The vending machine dangled crazily in the air. Freon gas hissed from the twin punctures, brown cola spewed across the floor. Far from satisfied, Jenkins immediately accelerated at top speed and rammed the Coke machine into the wall. The wall shuddered, the back wheels of the forklift bucked five inches in the air. The side panels popped off the battered vending machine, the crushed innards tumbled out the bottom. Grinding gears, Jenkins slammed the mangled Coke machine against the wall again and again.

"Goddammit, Jenkins!"

Dogshit Miller leaped onto the forklift and

ripped Jenkins out of the driver's seat. "What's wrong with you! Your pay's gonna be docked for this!"

"Don't touch me," Jenkins screamed, swinging his fists.

Dogshit ducked the blows and twisted Jenkins' arms behind his back. "You're paying for every penny, bastard!"

"Fuck off," Jenkins yelled, kicking at Dogshit's legs.

"You're off the job, you goddamn idiot!" Dogshit struggled to strengthen his grip. "You're outa work for two weeks!"

"Fuck off, Dogshit!" Jenkins kicked and struggled to free his arms. "You and the whole company —just fuck off!"

Dogshit finally got him in a hammerlock, almost breaking his neck, and marched him into the hallway. "Two weeks, you bastard shit. Every penny comes outa your goddamn paycheck."

Jenkins moaned with pain and kept kicking at him. When they reached the door, Dogshit looked back over his shoulder.

"Who the hell stopped the line? Hank, hit the button. Get that line moving!"

The workers stood in a sullen crowd, watching Dogshit shove Jenkins out onto the parking lot. The door slammed shut. They shuffled back toward the line, mumbling to each other.

"Fucking Dogshit, what does he care?"

"The bastards."

"They never fix nothing till somebody gets killed by it."

Hank walked to the button, then glanced at the others and shrugged as if to say, "What else can we do?" He pushed the button and the frames began moving down the line. The clock said fifteen minutes to closing time. The workers picked up their tools but just held them, looking at each other.

Suddenly Bobby Joe jumped up on a frame and shouted:

"Hey, you donkeys, you company-owned assholes! You gonna take that? Let's make us some lemons!"

"Right," Zeke shouted. "Let's get *down!* Let's screw 'em good!"

"Lemons, baby! This is the lemon line!"

"All right!"

The younger workers hooted with glee and plunged back into their jobs in a frenzy. Shouting encouragement, they worked faster than double-time. They installed two steering wheels in one frame, then three in the next. Clanking down the line came the glacial-blue frame, to which they attached the cranberry red doors, the sunflower yellow fenders, and a lime green trunk. Laughing, they shouted out imitations of Dogshit Miller.

"Keep her rolling, boys! Get off your butts, you kiss-ass monkeys!"

"Yessir, boss! I really do love my work now!"

"Ain't no slackers on the lemon line, Jack!"

The older workers backed away from the line and shook their heads, afraid of paycheck penalties and losing seniority.

"Dogshit ain't gonna like this," muttered Barney, the oldest black worker on the line.

Chicken Salad nodded. "Gonna be hell to pay tomorrow, I'll tell you. Sumabitch."

The younger workers responded by working even faster. Bobby Joe power-bolted the seats in

backward. Using two brushes, Zeke smeared glue all
over the windshields, the steering wheels, the control panels. Jerry welded the door seams so the
doors wouldn't open. Smokey welded shut the hoods
and trunks.

The older workers gradually got caught up in
the madcap mood and shouted encouragement from
the sidelines.

"Bust the shit outa that bitch!"

"Kick them bastards in the ass!"

Chicken Salad followed Zeke from frame to
frame, afraid to touch anything but talking incessantly.

"That's the stuff, Zeke. You forgot this part."

"Grab a brush, Chicken."

"Nah, I can't do this shit. I got eighteen years.
Hey, don't forget the windshield wipers. Sumabitch, ain't this something?"

Dogshit Miller returned with Clarence Hill.
They stopped in the doorway and stared at the
rainbow-colored monstrosities on the line. They
watched the workers grin at them innocently.

"See that, Clarence," Dogshit muttered. "See
what kinda morons you give us. Ain't gonna do
anything about it, are you?"

"What can anybody do?"

"Stop and forget it happened," Dogshit muttered, realizing things had gone too far for individual discipline. He punched the stop button.
"That's it, men. We're shutting down five minutes
early today."

"Whoopee!"

The workers streamed toward the locker room,
laughing and slapping each other on the back.

Six-thirty that evening, Jerry was eating supper at the kitchen table with Arlene and Bob, their eight-year-old son. Debby's seat was empty.

"Arlene," Jerry laughed, "you really shoulda seen it. Looked like King Kong had stomped on the whole line."

"Are you gonna get a discipline?"

"I don't care. I ain't felt this good since the Tigers won the Series."

"I want some more," Bob said, holding up his empty plate. "Can I have some of yours, Dad?"

Jerry reached for the box of Hamburger Helper and showed it to him. "Look, it says right here it's good for four helpings. 'Serves five.' You've had more than enough, Bob."

"I'm still hungry, Dad."

"Write the company."

"Can I have some of yours, Mom?"

"Have another piece of bread," she said.

"What about Debby's, Mom? She ain't ate anything."

"Where is Debby?" Jerry looked down the hallway and shouted, "Debby! Come to the table. Your food's getting cold."

"Honey," Arlene said uneasily, "don't be hard on her. She's had a rough day."

"What's wrong with her?"

"She doesn't feel good."

"Well, why not?" Jerry saw his daughter stick her head out of her bedroom door at the end of the hall. "Debby, come in here. What's wrong, honey?"

Arlene motioned for Jerry to get up and follow her. As they walked down the hall, Bob reached over and took some of his Dad's Hamburger Helper.

"What's wrong with her, Arlene? How come nobody ever tells me anything?"

"Honey, you remember how she wanted to be on the baton-twirling team?"

"Yeah." Jerry saw the drops of blood on his daughter's lips. "What happened, Debby?"

She didn't answer. He opened his daughter's mouth and saw her gums were cut and blood red.

"She tried to make braces out of a coat hanger," Arlene said.

"Jesus Christ," Jerry said, stunned. He tried to embrace Debby, but she turned and ran into her bedroom, slamming the door behind her.

"Jesus Christ, Arlene. Get those goddamn braces, and get 'em tomorrow."

"But we can't afford 'em, honey."

"Screw it. We'll worry about the bill when it comes."

"Maybe we can have another garage sale."

"Shit, what we got to sell?"

Arlene put her head on his shoulder. "It'll work out, honey."

Jerry held her in his arms and stared at his daughter's bedroom door, his face looking like a man locked behind bars for life. "Just get them braces."

An hour later Jerry walked into Oogie's. He had to get out of the house. He spotted Zeke and Smokey at a corner table and joined them.

"Bartowski," Zeke said, laughing. "Foxy chick here looking for you earlier. Hot pants, fancy wig, big boots—just your type."

"Yeah," Smokey smiled. "We told her you was welding shut doors."

Jerry sat down without really listening to them.

"Look," he said seriously, "I been thinking about what you guys were talking about. You really gonna do it?"

"Maybe," Smokey shrugged. "Yeah, I guess we are."

"Smokey knows a girl that used to work for Bald Eddie," Zeke said. "She's coming over to his place tomorrow night."

"You gonna carry roscoes?"

"No," Smokey said. "No guns. It's just a breaking and entering. Better be grand larceny too."

"How much you think there could be?"

"Four or five grand," Zeke said. "What do you say?"

"Nah. It ain't for me."

"Like Smoke says, it's just a B and E. Gonna be a pushover."

"Oh, you'll pull it off all right. It just ain't for me."

Jerry got up and walked across the room to the bar.

Oogie said, "Beer, Jerry?"

"And bourbon by."

7

The next evening Zeke was at Smokey's apartment for their meeting. The red party lights had been replaced by regular light bulbs. Zeke sat at the dining table across from Maxine, an attractive young black woman wearing finely tailored clothes. Zeke was sketching a floor plan, while she described the layout of union headquarters.

"No, that's a wall," she said. "The counter's here, and this should be two rooms."

"Like this?"

"Right, with windows here."

Smokey suddenly approached them from the bedroom, speaking on a telephone with a long cord. He looked at Maxine and said, "I got Charlie T. on the line. He wants to know what color the lettering is. You know, the word 'Safewell'?"

"Gold, I think. Maybe yellow."

"Gold, maybe yellow," Smokey said into the phone. After listening a minute, he cupped his hand over the receiver and looked at Zeke.

"Charlie says it's probably a '46 or '47. Suggests we drill and pick it. Take about thirty minutes. He'll show us how."

"Okay," Zeke said. "How much does he want?"

"A hundred bucks now, and then ten percent of the take."

"You got a hundred?"

"Fuck no," Smokey shrugged. "I shot everything up my nose last weekend."

"Shit, that does it. I got about ten bucks."

"I only got twenty-five." Smokey looked at his diamond ring as if he could never part with it. "Fuck, I guess I could pawn this. Just pay me off the top."

"Great. Tell the man he's got a deal."

As Smokey resumed his phone conversation, Zeke examined his sketch again, wondering what would happen to his family if he got arrested. This shit was a sucker's game, and it was getting for real. But the tax shit was no different. Once the money trouble got serious, your ass was in the coffin. Like when Arthur got all them hospital bills and it wasn't a year before his kids were in goddamn foster homes.

There was a knock at the front door and Zeke motioned for Maxine to answer it. She opened the door and saw Jerry peering over the chain latch.

"Hi," he said. "Is Smokey home?"

"Who wants to know?"

"Bartowski, come on in," Zeke said. "It's okay, Maxine."

"Hey, Zeke."

Jerry walked to the table, unzipping his Bardohl jacket and revealing his Farrah Fawcett T-shirt.

"I was just in the neighborhood. Thought I'd drop by."

"Grab a chair."

"This the floor plan?"

"Yeah. Here's the safe."

Leaning over the table, Jerry examined the sketch and wondered if it really was a way out. He remembered his drunken father always saying, "I'm a man living in hell and there ain't no way out." Well, what was this? A road map to the bank, or a fast ticket to the pen? Didn't make much difference, for Chrissakes. He was so money-short that his own daughter was mutilating herself. Besides, it was his money in the first place, wasn't it?

"Have a seat, Jerry." Smokey hung up the phone and took a chair at the table. "You want in?"

"I'm just curious. What've you got?"

"What do you wanna know?"

Jerry removed his jacket and sat down, saying, "I wanna hear everything. Run through it from the top."

The next day the three men met after work in Oogie's parking lot and drove to downtown Detroit in Smokey's "pimpmobile," a candy-red Continental with silver pinstripes.

Parking across the street from union headquarters, they surveyed the bland brick building. The street wasn't busy and the building seemed almost deserted in the orangeish afternoon sunlight.

Smokey was professionally calm while Zeke popped his fingers with nervous excitement, his eyes constantly darting up and down the street. Damn, this shit was getting for real. Jerry bit a fingernail, wincing at the thought of being arrested. Damn, what if Arlene found out?

"Damn," Jerry muttered. "What about the rollers?"

"It's the D.P.D.," Smokey said. "At night they got a squad car passing by every fifteen minutes. The security guard comes in every hour and checks it out. Usually about quarter past the hour."

"Do they have any of that TV shit?"

"What TV shit?"

"Them closed-circuit camera things."

"No. Just an electric-eye alarm."

"Damn," Zeke said. "I saw that in *The Pink Panther*. Those muthas be rough, Jack. The minute you step on the floor, they can tell how much you weigh, whether you a man or woman, how old—"

"Fuck it," Smokey said. "This just be an electric eye on the door. Like at the supermarket."

"Yeah? Well, whose car we gonna use? Mine got funky again."

"We can use mine," Smokey said, tapping his fur-covered dashboard.

Jerry laughed with scorn and said, "You kidding? Use this pussywagon? The cops'll spot this showboat clear across Lake Huron."

"So let's use yours," Zeke said.

"Nah. Needs a new gas pump."

"So get one," Smokey said. "Needs a new everything."

65

"Okay. But then maybe I should get some more money."

"Fuck it," Smokey said. "Get off that shit, Jerry. We're all in even."

"Yeah, okay. Do we need any masks or anything —for disguises?"

"Maybe," Smokey shrugged. "Just in case."

"Okay, I think we should. We can use bandanas or something."

"No way, sucker," Zeke said. "When I get arrested, I ain't gonna look like no goddamn cowboy."

"You get 'em, Zeke," Smokey said. "Halloween masks or stuff like that. Crazy shit that'd make anybody forget our faces."

Suddenly a Buick stopped in front of the building. Janet walked out of the building and handed the driver an envelope. The driver nodded and pulled away.

"Duck down," Zeke said. "Who's in that Buick?"

They all slouched down until the Buick passed by, then watched Janet walk back into the building.

"That's her, Smoke," Zeke said. "The fox I was telling you about. Bald Eddie's secretary."

"I seen her before," Smokey said. "She ain't that good-looking."

"You crazy? What happened to your taste, brother? The lady's a fox!"

"Shit, you think every chick's a fox. That bitch is a bow-wow. She eats Gainesburgers."

"Sounds like you already tried it, brother."

Jerry sat and stared at them with increasing concern. Jesus, what am I doing here with these two fuck-offs?

The next day each man prepared for their midnight rendezvous. During lunch break Jerry ate with Jan Budziszewski in the repair shop. They had been hunting partners since high school and agreed to skip work again on the first day of deer season.

Jerry said, "Your rifle still working?"

"Sure is, old buddy."

"That was a helluva discount I got for you, Jan. And on those twin Mercs for your outboard."

"The kids love it," Jan nodded. "Was that stuff 'hot,' Jerry?"

"You kidding? I don't mess with shit like that."

"Sure. I just wondered why the serial numbers was scratched off, you know?"

Jerry smiled. "I was just doing you a favor, Jan. Now I want one myself."

"Sure, old buddy."

Jerry returned to his place on the line, leaving his lunch bucket with Jan and telling him where his car was parked. At quitting time Jerry walked out to his car and found the lunch bucket under his seat. Instead of going to Oogie's, he drove to the Total gas station where he worked and parked in back. He opened his lunch bucket, removed a new gas pump, and began installing it.

Zeke was browsing through the toy section of a dime store. He selected some eyeglasses with pop-out eyeballs, a pair of buck teeth, two beanie caps, one with propellers and the other with an arrow through the head.

A little boy walked up to him and said, "Hey, man. Can you spare a quarter?"

"Yeah," Zeke said, pulling a ten-dollar bill from his pocket. "You got change for a ten?"

"No."

"Sorry, catch you later."

Smokey walked out of a pawn shop with two hundred twenty dollars for his diamond ring and strode down the sidewalk. Slim, a young black, was leaning against a parked car with twenty-five wristwatches strapped on one arm.

"Smokey, my man."

"Hey, Slim."

"You want some watches? Got a great deal for you, Smoke. Sixteen jewels, gold-plated. Made by Bulova. Over the counter these suckers sell for a hundred ten dollars."

Smokey looked at two of the watches. "It don't say 'Bulova.'"

"It's made under a different name, you know?"

"I'll give you fifteen bucks."

"Twenty."

"Fifteen bucks, for three of 'em."

"What kinda shit is that, brother? What kinda fool you think I am?"

Smokey started to walk away.

"Not so fast, brother. You got a deal."

Jerry picked up Smokey shortly before midnight, then drove over to Zeke's house. Smokey had a small toolbox containing a drill and picks. Jerry had a pillowcase for the money. They both wore dark clothes and work gloves.

Waiting in the front seat, they watched Zeke quietly shut his front door and tiptoe to the car. He carried a brown paper bag of disguises.

When he got into the back seat, the three men looked at each other for a moment as they sat silently in the darkness. Finally Smokey said, "Everybody set?"

Zeke and Jerry nodded nervously.

"Synchronize your watches. It's 11:56."

"I ain't got a watch," Zeke whispered.

Jerry nodded. "Mine's broke."

"You're in luck," Smokey said, handing each a watch. "I got a couple of great hot ones today. Sixteen jewels, gold-plated. Only ten bucks each."

"Pay you later," Zeke mumbled, strapping it on. "Let's get outa here before Carolyn wakes up."

Jerry quietly revved the motor and pulled away in his beat-up gray Ford with one blue door. The gas pump was working fine. Riding in silence, they took the Edsel Ford Freeway to the Chrysler Freeway, then drove down the third exit ramp. The dark streets had almost no traffic.

Jerry stopped in front of union headquarters and cut the headlights. The only sound was their motor idling in the quiet night air. Jerry backed into the parking lot across the dark street and parked between two empty cars. They stared through the windshield at the dark brick building. There wasn't another person in sight.

"Guard's already gone," Smokey said. "Checked it out ten minutes ago."

They watched the building and waited. Jerry nervously tapped his gloved hands on the steering wheel. Zeke kept glancing up and down the street, then finally said, "Where are they?"

"Be cool," Smokey said calmly.

"Shit," Zeke muttered, still uptight. "Maybe we should just hit a liquor store like everybody else."

"You kidding?" Jerry stopped tapping. "Hell, I'd never do a *real* robbery."

"What do you call this?"

"Getting back," Jerry said firmly.

"Shit, honky. Tell that to the rollers. They'll stick a merit badge up your ass."

"Here they come," Smokey whispered.

Quickly ducking down, they watched the Detroit Police Department patrol car come slowly down the street. The two D.P.D. officers in the blue and white car glanced at the Headquarters building, then slowly drove out of sight.

"Let's do it," Smokey said. "Put your gloves on."

Jerry started the motor and drove slowly down the dark empty street. Turning the corner, they pulled into the alley and parked behind the brick building.

Wearing crepe-soled shoes, they stepped quietly from the car and glanced around in the darkness. The only sound came from the deisel trucks on the distant freeway. They walked across the asphalt to the rear door. Their dark clothes made them barely visible against the dark brick building.

Smokey crouched beside the metal door. Taking a small crowbar from his tool kit, he began to jimmy the lock. Zeke clutched his brown paper bag and watched. Jerry tucked the pillowcase under his belt. Suddenly Smokey swung open the door and they gazed into the dark hallway.

"Looks like nobody's home," Jerry said.

Grabbing a handful of sand, Smokey tossed it into the doorway. The dust revealed the reddish light beam, crossing the doorway at thigh level.

"There's the electric eyes," Smokey said.

One by one, they crawled on their hands and knees under the thin reddish beam. Zeke reached back over the beam and quietly closed the door.

Smokey flicked on his penlight and led them down the hallway. Moving slowly, they passed the darkened offices and entered the main reception room. Smokey ran the penlight along the wall until it found the huge door of the walk-in safe.

"There she be," Zeke whispered. "What a big, beautiful—"

Zeke's foot kicked over a metal wastebasket with a loud clang, sending the contents spilling across the floor. Everybody froze in their tracks.

"Take it slow," Smokey said.

"Jesus," Jerry muttered. "I think I'm having cardiac arrest."

Slowly they tiptoed to the huge black metal door, the penlight flashing on the gold word "Safewell." Smokey handed Zeke the light and opened his tool kit for the electric drill.

Zeke whispered, "You got the diagram?"

"Here," Smokey said, fitting a bit into his drill.

Zeke unfolded the paper diagram and placed it against the door, the cut-out hole slipping snugly around the combination lock. Three black dots circled the combination. Charlie T. had notated each dot with instructions on how and when to drill. Zeke taped the paper in place.

Jerry tested the safe handle. It turned freely in his hand. He squinted at the handle, wondering if it was supposed to move like that.

Plugging in the cord, Smokey wrapped his

71

jacket around the drill to muffle the sound. Then he turned it on and immediately began drilling the first hole.

Jerry moved the handle again and whispered in Smokey's ear. "Hey, Smoke."

Smokey continued drilling. "What?"

"I think it's open."

"Huh?" Smokey turned off the drill and stood up.

"The safe. It's open."

Jerry pushed down the handle and pulled open the heavy door, ripping the paper diagram in half.

"Holy fuck," Smokey said.

They walked silently into the huge dark safe, Zeke flashing the shelves with the penlight. The shelves were empty except for a few files, stacks of leaflets, and a box of political buttons.

"Hell," Jerry muttered, "no wonder it's a knock-over. They don't keep nothing in here."

"That can't be," Zeke mumbled. Spotting a white paper bag, he stuck his hand inside and pulled out a half-eaten sandwich. "Somebody's goddamn lunch."

Jerry paged through some files. "This is stupid. Let's get the hell outa here."

"Wait," Smokey said. "There's a safe over here, down in the corner."

"That's it," Zeke said happily, flashing his light on the small portable safe. "That's where all the money be, Jack."

Jerry tested the lock. "How we gonna open it?"

"We'll torch it later," Smokey said.

Suddenly there was a bang on the front door. They all froze and listened: it sounded like somebody turning a key in the lock.

Zeke whispered, "Who's that?"

"Maybe the guard," Jerry whispered. "What time is it?"

Smokey glanced at his watch. "It's one forty-five."

"I got twelve fifty-eight," Zeke whispered.

"Mine's stopped," Jerry muttered.

They heard the front door open. Zeke flipped off the penlight. Smokey walked to the heavy safe door and closed it until there was only a two-inch crack.

Staring through the crack, they watched a security guard enter the reception area and shine his flashlight around the walls. He spotted the wastebasket and set it upright. Glancing at the safe, he walked quickly to the phone and began dialing.

Jerry whispered in Smokey's ear: "What we gonna do?"

"Run for it," Smokey whispered. "Get out them disguises."

Zeke nodded. Opening the brown paper bag, he handed a disguise to Jerry and put one on Smokey. Lifting the drill next to his ear, Smokey stared intently at the guard waiting for somebody to answer his call. Fucker was calling the rollers. Fuck it, now or never.

Holding the drill like a club, Smokey kicked open the heavy door.

The guard looked up and for one moment he saw the motley trio approaching him from the safe. But he couldn't believe what his eyes saw: a huge black man with whirligig eyeglasses and a power drill, a stocky white man with a portable safe and an arrow through his head, and a wiry black man with gigantic buck teeth and a propeller beanie.

Smokey swung the drill at the side of his head

and coldcocked him. His body slumped to the floor. Zeke and Jerry stared at him, frozen with disbelief.

Wrapping the cord around the drill, Smokey walked to his tool kit. "Got the safe?"

"Yeah."

"Let's go. Don't leave nothin' behind."

They hustled down the dark hallway, the portable safe banging against Jerry's leg. Zeke stuffed their disguises in his paper bag with the diagram.

"Guard ain't dead, is he, Smoke?"

"No way."

"You sure?"

"It's just assault and battery."

Zeke opened the rear door. They glanced up and down the alley, then headed for the car.

Thirty minutes later the car was parked inside the gas station where Jerry worked. While Zeke and Smokey watched, Jerry cut open the metal safe with the blow torch. Blue light flickered across their impatient faces and the stacked auto parts. Finishing, Jerry pulled off his goggles and cut the hissing flame. The cooling red-hot metal darkened quickly but continued to smoke.

Zeke said, "Hope you didn't burn the big green, sucker."

"Let's find out."

Jerry opened the small safe and dumped its contents across the workbench. "It's just more papers," he muttered disgustedly. There was nothing but six blue accounting books, a green notebook, and a manila envelope. No greenbacks at all.

Smokey grabbed the manila envelope and read the markings on the back: "3/$100s, 15/$20s." He opened it and began counting the bills, muttering, "Goddamn petty cash."

"There's gotta be more," Zeke said, leafing through the accounting books.

"This is chickenshit," Jerry muttered.

"Six hundred," Smokey announced, finishing his re-count.

"At least it's grand larceny," Zeke said sarcastically.

"At least it's something," Jerry said. "Split it."

"Okay," Smokey said, "there's a hundred for Charlie T., plus sixty for his ten percent. That leaves four forty, which is a hundred forty bucks apiece."

Jerry took his money, grumbling, "To think I risked my ass for this chickenshit."

Zeke stared at his hundred forty dollars, wondering what to do about the tax man. This shit wouldn't pay the goddamn late penalty.

Smokey held up the last bill. "Plus an extra twenty."

"That's to pay for the disguises," Zeke said.

"No," Jerry said. "I need money for the gas pump."

"I'll keep it," Smokey said. "You guys owe me twenty for the watches."

"Watches!" Zeke ripped off his watch. "You can keep the goddamn watches, Jack!"

"Okay," Smokey said. "We'll throw fingers. Odd man wins."

Smokey counted to three, his voice echoing through the suddenly quiet station. They thrust out their fingers and Zeke won.

"That wasn't fair," Jerry said. "Zeke went late."

75

"Bullshit! I went first! Zeke the freak Brown always gets down!"

"Wasn't fair. We gotta do it again."

"It was fair," Smokey said. "What we gonna do with the safe?"

"Can't stay here," Jerry said. "Station gonna open soon."

"I'll take care of it," Zeke said. "There's a garbage dump by my brother's place."

8

Newspaper and TV reporters crowded into the outer office of union headquarters and stuck their microphones in Bald Eddie's face. He stood like a bulldog in front of the safe door, deftly fielding their questions under the harsh spotlights. Beside him stood Clarence Hill, lawyers, and assistants.

One reporter said, "We hear the door to the safe was open. Is that true?"

"I can't say at this time," Bald Eddie said. "The police are looking into it."

"How much was taken?"

"We're still trying to determine that."

"We heard it was ten grand. Is that right?"

"Yes," Bald Eddie said, glancing at his chief lawyer. "You could say that."

Jerry was waiting for customers at the gas station, when he saw the interview on the six-thirty TV newscast. Goddamn liars, he thought. You could say ten grand! What ten fucking grand? What the hell was Bald Eddie talking about?

He sipped his coffee, then suddenly grew extremely tense as another reporter announced an interview with "the only man who actually saw the Oreo Gang."

The security guard was sitting in a hospital bed with a bandage around his forehead. "It was crazy," he said. "They just came right out of the safe. Two black guys with a white one in the middle. Like an Oreo."

"What did the blacks look like?"

"I really don't know. They had disguises."

"What about the white man?"

The guard thought about it, then shrugged and said, "He had an arrow through his head."

Jerry sighed so hard with relief that he spilled coffee on his pants. Shit, saved by the golden arrow.

An hour later, when Jerry had pulled on his Bardohl jacket, turned off the station lights and was just stepping outside to lock the pumps, Burrows pulled up and stepped out of his unmarked government-issue Ford.

"Five dollars unleaded," he said, glancing at the darkened station. "Closing up early, Jerry?"

"Yeah," Jerry said, unhooking the pump and wondering how much Burrows knew. "Going bowling."

"With who?"

"My friend."

"What friend?"

"You know. Zeke."

"Oh," Burrows said, pausing for effect. "The black guy. You got *two* black friends, right?"

Jerry glared at him coldly, his voice cold as steel, "Want me to check the oil?"

"No," Burrows said, egging him.

"Then what the hell *do* you want?"

Burrows shrugged, then suddenly looked straight into Jerry's eyes. "I suppose you heard about the union robbery. Ten thousand dollars. Really something, ain't it? Who would've thought they had so much money in there?"

Jerry shrugged calmly and said, "I don't know nothin' about it."

"All I know is what I read in the papers," Burrows said with feigned innocence.

"Then you know more than me. Ain't got time to read no papers." Jerry pulled out the nozzle and capped the tank. "That'll be five bucks."

Shaking his head ruefully, Burrows handed him a five-dollar bill. "Everything's a rip-off, ain't it? Five bucks for two bucks' worth of gas."

Jerry took the money and locked the pump, saying, "It's those fucking camel jockeys."

"What?"

"The fucking A-rabs."

Burrows smiled, then opened his car door and looked back at Jerry. "Well, if you ever have anything to talk about, don't be afraid to come to me. See me first, Jerry. I ain't with these local or state cops. You don't know it yet, but I'm your friend. I'll do right by you. I just wanna see your union set straight."

Jerry stared at him but didn't say a word.

"Well, have a good time bowling."

Jerry watched him get back into the car and drive away, then he locked the second pump. What the hell? These government shits knew what you were doing before you did it. Pecking at your ass like goddamn vultures.

Zeke sat on his sofa and finished reading the short article in the *Detroit Free Press.* The two-column headline was near the bottom of the front page: OREO GANG NETS 10G IN UNION THEFT. He tossed the paper on the floor, wondering who was robbing who. Ain't no magic that's changing six Ben Franklins into ten thousand Washingtons. Ain't no Oreo Gang that's making the *real* theft, Jack.

Carolyn leaned against his shoulder, watching *Good Times* on TV and laughing at Jimmy Walker. "He's so funny," she said.

"Shit, woman. You think that's funny? I'll show you what *real* fun is."

"Oh, shut up."

Zeke smiled and sipped his Stroh's. Then he picked up the union's green notebook and absent-mindedly leafed through the pages, wondering what the tax man's notebook looked like. Fucking government owned more of your ass than you did. Fuckers had a mortgage on your whole life. Always too busy to give you the time of day, but never too busy to take the coins from your pocket and charge a goddamn penalty besides.

Suddenly Zeke noticed the high interest rates in the notebook and examined the coded entries more closely.

6-21-77 2500 to RG via Tim at 15% per mon.
         Confirm 7-21-77
6-27-77 Rec 500 from McG via Greek. Outstan:
         15G by 8-1-77
7-12-77 5G to Lake via JB. Total outstan: 45G
         at 18% per mon.

Carolyn switched off the TV and headed toward the bedroom, saying, "Hurry up, honey. We've only got five minutes."

Zeke nodded without listening. He scanned the notebook entries and wondered where they could lead. Lotsa sharks in these waters, Jack. Enough interest to buy a train ticket to the promised land of broken promises. Shit, enough to buy the whole goddamn train.

Thirty minutes later they were in the bowling alley. Carolyn and Arlene sat at the scoring table, while Zeke and Jerry drank beer on the bench behind them. The kids were playing in the pinball room.

Jerry sipped his Stroh's and muttered, "Ten fucking grand. Those fuckers would choke on the truth. They get so used to lying they can't do nothing else."

Zeke nodded, then shouted as Carolyn got a strike. "My woman getting down tonight! Carolyn be hitting those pins, Jack!"

Carolyn smiled. "Nothing to it."

As Arlene selected her ball, Zeke whispered to Jerry, "You know that stuff we found in the safe?"

"I thought you threw that shit out."

"I kept a notebook. There's something funny in it."

"Like what?"

Arlene missed her spare and Carolyn said, "Your turn, Zeke. Get a spare and we go ahead."

"Say what, woman? A spare? Shit, this gonna be a strike or Stevie Wonder don't need no cane." Zeke threw his ball down the lane and dropped three pins.

Carolyn looked at Arlene and shook her head. "Sometimes he can be so damn slow."

Arlene shrugged. "At least we get out once in a while."

"Yes," Carolyn sighed. "Otherwise, they just go out and get drunk. Or they try to play dice with the midnight mice."

"Like they say, Carolyn. Boys that work hard got a right to play hard."

"We work hard too, Arlene."

"I know," Arlene nodded. "I try not to think about it. He does his best. He takes pretty good care of us."

Zeke threw his second ball and knocked down two more pins.

Carolyn said, "Don't you aim at all?"

"Hush you mouth. I'm just getting warmed up." Zeke grabbed his beer and sat down, muttering, "White folks musta invented this game."

Jerry said, "Like what was funny?"

"It's a list of loans," Zeke whispered. "But they ain't regular loans. They're all at shark rates."

"Jesus, we better tell Smokey."

At ten o'clock Smokey was leafing through the green spiral notebook on his dining table, stopping to read several entries carefully.

Zeke smiled wryly from across the table, still wearing his green bowling shirt. Jerry paced around the table in his yellow Stroh's T-shirt, biting a fingernail.

"Shit," Smokey finally said. "This ain't no big deal."

"But it *is* illegal," Zeke said.

"So what ain't?"

"Michigan National don't charge no fifteen and twenty percent a month."

"So it's illegal. So what?"

"Don't you see, sucker? This be what those government guys been talking about. Illegal loans from the union's pension fund."

"Yeah," Smokey nodded. "Probably through Vegas."

"Now you talking," Zeke smiled. "I thought you'd be interested."

Jerry stopped pacing and sat down. "What do you mean? What is this shit anyway?"

"Dynamite," Zeke said. "We finally got them where they've always had us—by the balls. We got what that government guy's looking for, proof of the union's fucking corruption. We can throw all those bastards out. Hill, Bald Eddie, all of 'em. Bring the muthafuckers down."

"Holy shit," Jerry said, standing up again. "We're in trouble now. They're gonna really be after us. Pope couldn't save our ass now."

"You crazy? This is our chance to change the union."

"You kidding, Zeke? Screw that stuff. This is the worst thing that coulda happened to us. We gotta get rid of that book fast. Pretend it never existed."

"You're both fucking crazy," Smokey said.

"What?"

"Neither of you knows shit about how things go down."

"I suppose you do," Zeke said.

"Why do you go to the line every Friday?"

Zeke and Jerry shrugged.

"Cuz the finance man gonna come to your house Saturday, right?"

"Yeah."

Smokey stood up and put his foot on his chair. "You see, that's the way they got it set up. You gotta dig that fact. Everything the company does is meant to keep us on the line. To keep us broke with just enough money to pay last week's bills, but not this week's bills. Otherwise nobody'd be crazy enough to go back to the line. Everything they do, the way they pit lifers against newboys, the old against the young, the black against the white, is meant to keep us in our place."

Zeke stood up, tapping the green notebook. "This'll put them in their place."

"Politics don't change shit. Only thing that makes any difference is money. Money makes us free. When you got the money, you can fuck the man, you can just take off and do what you please. You're free."

"But I *want* those bastards busted," Zeke said. "Especially Clarence muthafucking Hill."

"That's your problem," Smokey said. "You're thinking of hurting them instead of helping yourself."

Zeke glared angrily. "You an analyst now?"

Jerry stopped pacing and said, "So how do we help ourselves?"

"Blackmail," Smokey said. "They want this book, they'll pay for it. We'll get the ten grand those ratfuckers are getting from the insurance company."

"Jesus," Jerry said, pacing again. "It's just gonna get us in more trouble."

Zeke walked across the room, realizing Smokey was right. Clarence could wait. The tax man came first.

Smokey walked to his bar and poured a glass of bourbon. Then he took a drink and watched the other two nervously pacing the room, giving them time to think it over. Fucking union would play dirty pool to the end. Bald Eddie would shoot all his guns and dump all his shit. But ten grand makes you forget an awful lot of shit.

Jerry stopped at the window and stared down at the dark street, wishing the whole mess would just go away. Their asses were in the grinder already. But ten grand wasn't chickenfeed.

Zeke climbed on a bar stool and said, "Okay, how would we do it?"

"Easy," Smokey said. "Send Bald Eddie a Xerox page from the notebook. Tell him what we want. If he wants to pay, have him put an ad in the *Free Press.*"

"What if they won't pay?"

"Then we do what you want, Zeke. Turn 'em in and bring 'em down."

Jerry joined them at the bar and said, "Do you think they'll really pay, Smoke?"

"Let's find out."

9

Arlene packed the sandwiches neatly in Jerry's lunch bucket and glanced at him with a worried frown. He sat motionless in his chair, staring blankly at his scrambled eggs. During breakfast he always grumbled about the plant or his health, but today he didn't move a muscle. He hadn't even touched his coffee.

She looked perky in her puffed blond hairdo, because she always tried to be presentable, even in the morning. But Jerry looked awful. The dark circles under his eyes made him look like a sick dog. She joined him at the table and patted her hair, wondering what to say. She couldn't tell if he was going to explode or stumble back to bed.

"Your coffee's getting cold."

He said nothing.

"Something wrong, honey?"

"No," he muttered without looking up.

"You haven't touched your eggs."

"Yeah."

"What's wrong?"

"Nothing."

"Well, why don't you eat something?"

"Goddammit, Arlene!" He pounded the table, shouting, "Can't you see I'm thinking? Can't I even think around here anymore?"

"I'm just trying to help."

"Sorry. Just leave me alone."

"Okay. Maybe you should stay home today. You don't look so good, you know?"

"Smart, Arlene. That's really smart. If I stay home, who's gonna pay all the bills? Who's gonna pay for the house and the music lessons and all the other chickenshit?"

"I didn't know it was so bad. I could try to get a part-time job."

"No, don't start that stuff again. Everything's okay. Just let me think."

"Debby's supposed to get her braces fitted today. I was gonna take her after school, but I could cancel the appointment."

"No. Get the best ones they got."

"I should get my hair done too. If we can afford it?"

"Of course," Jerry sighed, rubbing his stiff muscles. "Sorry I shouted at you, honey. Got a lot on my mind."

"It's something at the plant, ain't it?"

"Yeah."

"Don't worry. It'll work out."

"Yeah."

"What do you think? Should I do my hair like Farrah Fawcett?"

"Leave me alone, Arlene."

"Okay," she said, walking to the counter to make breakfast for the kids.

Jerry picked up his cup and stared at the black coffee, wondering how badly he'd get burned. Bald Eddie wouldn't take this shit lying down. Bastard had busted ass before. He'd grind the Oreo Gang into Hamburger Helper and kick the pieces to kingdom come. You couldn't turn back, but you could get it over. If he paid, fine. If he didn't, fine. Just unload the damn notebook and go back to work.

Carolyn placed the coffee thermos in Zeke's lunch bucket, then walked to the table and poured another cup for him. He was a twitching wind-up toy, his fork arranging and rearranging the omelet, his shoe tapping the floor. Usually he had eaten breakfast and driven all the way to work before he was really awake. But today he was wide-eyed and churning. He'd gulped six cups of coffee already and his cup was empty again.

She joined him at the table and poured another cup, wondering what to say. He was burning on a very short fuse.

"What's the trouble, honey?"

"Everything."

"The tax man?"

"It's all them bastards, Carolyn. They put a hurting on my ass, but I ain't gonna take this shit much longer."

"Who is it this time, Zeke? Is it Dogshit or Clarence?"

"It's every last one of them bastards. It's becoming so clear to me, now that I finally got a chance."

"We could get a loan for the tax money."

"You crazy? I ain't swimming with no sharks. I seen *Jaws*. Those suckers be taking everything."

"We'll find a way, honey."

"Maybe I already did. Ain't gonna be easy, but Zeke Brown is finished with the ass-kissing. Bet on it."

"What're you talking about?"

"I ain't sure, but maybe I can get off the line."

"Oh, honey, are you serious?"

"Don't be getting excited," Zeke laughed. "I got a long way to go, so just let me think about it. Got my lunch ready?"

"Almost."

"Well, get moving."

Zeke poured another cup of coffee and took a long sip. This time things gonna change, he thought. I'm gonna make them fuckers pay one way or another. I may hafta stay on the line and I may hafta keep eating shit, but it's damn well gonna be a better class of shit. No more of this heavy shit for Zeke Brown. Bet on that, Jack.

Zeke and Jerry met in the parking lot, walking toward the drab gray plant under the bleak smoggy sky. They walked toward the small door under the big signboard that said: BETTER CARS FOR BETTER AMERICANS.

"Hey, Jerry. What's happening?"

"Jesus, you're wide awake. What's wrong?"

"I'm a killer today, Jack. Anybody stepping on me is stepping on a bomb."

"You ain't drunk, are you?"

"Shit, no."

"Well, I am," Jerry said, showing the pint of Jim Beam in his pocket. "Stopped off for this on the way down. I wanna talk to you."

"About what?"

"About everything. I'm getting worried."

"Stay cool, Jerry. It's just the waiting game."

"I don't know, man. This shit's getting very heavy. You think Smokey's right? Think we can pull it off?"

"Cool out, man. Bald Eddie's the one who's supposed to be worrying. Not us. Fucker's probably pulling out the last of his short hairs right now."

"Yeah," Jerry smiled. "I'd sure like to see that."

"Now you talking."

"So you really think we can do it?"

Zeke lowered his voice, speaking seriously. "I don't know if we gonna do the ten grand, but we're damn well gonna do *some*-thing. Bet on that shit, brother."

"I hope so, Zeke. Hell, I just wish it was over."

"See that," Zeke said, pointing at the signboard on the roof. "When this is over, that's what we're gonna be. Goddamn better Americans. One way or another, we're gonna be walking down Money Street."

"Shit," Jerry laughed. "I ain't gonna feel better if you start talking crazy talk."

They finally crossed the huge parking lot and entered the dark cavernous building. The line was quiet but yesterday's stench still hung in the air. Glancing down the endless line, they entered the locker room. Zeke opened his broken locker handle with a ball-point pen. Jerry stuck his earplugs in his pocket, then filled his nostrils with nasal spray.

"Give me a hit of that stuff," Zeke said.

"Help yourself," Jerry muttered. "Bastard politicians always bitching about air pollution in the great outdoors. The shitheads oughta take a whiff of the cancer soup in here."

They both took a slug from the Jim Beam. Then they trudged to their positions just as the line started and the pounding metal presses began shaking the concrete floor.

Dogshit Miller had a manpower shortage in the afternoon. He needed the workhorse of the plant. He strode down the line, searching for Smokey and calling out, "Utility man!"

Smokey was bolting seats with a power wrench. He heard Dogshit approaching but didn't look up.

"Hey, utility man!"

Smokey kept working.

"Don't give me a hard time, Smoke."

Smokey climbed inside the car and power-bolted the back seats.

"Okay, okay," Dogshit said, sticking his head inside the car. "You win. I would like your attention, Mr. Smokey James."

Smokey climbed out of the car and nodded.

"We need another man in frame welding." Dogshit said.

"Why?"

"Don't give me a hard time. Just get down there."

"What happened?"

"Two guys on sick leave, another just passed out. Gone for the day. Now get moving. They're falling way behind."

Smokey shrugged. "Sounds like I'll be doing the

work of three men. Maybe I should get triple-time pay."

"I'm not gonna go through this again," Dogshit warned, shaking his finger. "Now get moving or get off the line."

Smokey glared into his eyes until he stopped shaking his finger, then strolled up the line toward frame welding.

Dogshit strode down the line, looking for slouchers to vent his anger on. "Keep her moving, Flannigan."

"I'm doing my best," Flannigan said.

"Well, do better. I should get my mother down here. She'd put you boys to shame." He spotted Jerry using hs nasal spray and shouted, "Blow your nose on your own time, Bartowski."

Jerry flipped down his helmet and shot off a burst of sparks. He'd been getting angrier all day. He'd tried to make the time go faster by concentrating on his favorite fantasy, imagining himself married to his high school dream Penny Holmes, going with her to funky movies and classy restaurants and then to their big brass bed. But all he could see was the fat ugly face of Bald Eddie Johnson.

Dogshit Miller kept striding down the line and spotted Zeke working glue-and-rubber on windshields with Chicken Salad O'Neill and the old old black worker Barney Ward. Lazy niggers, he thought, they're always dragging. He stopped beside Zeke and said, "Get a move on, Brown. You're dragging. You're always dragging the line."

"Sumabitch," Chicken Salad said. "We work as fast as we can."

"Did I ask you?"

Chicken Salad looked down, mumbling to himself.

Zeke continued working and said, "Get off my back."

Dogshit started to walk away and said flatly, "Shut up and work, Brown."

Zeke stopped working and said, "Get off my case, Miller."

Dogshit turned around, strode back toward Zeke, and snapped angrily, "Watch out, Zeke. Any more lip from you and you'll be another donkey in the street. I'll dock your pay for the day."

Zeke shouted, his body shaking with anger, "Get off my ass, Dogshit! I'm warning you, peckerwood! This shit stops right here!"

"That's it! You're through!"

"I'm a killer!" Zeke grabbed a power wrench and thrust it within an inch of Dogshit's face. "No more shit or I'll break a wrench over your goddamn head!"

"You're off the line!" Dogshit backed away and called up the line, "Super! Super! Jimmy, get the superintendent!"

Nobody went to get the super, so Dogshit stomped up the line to find him, muttering, "We've got no time for smart-ass niggers."

"Muthafucker," Zeke shouted back.

The three workers watched Dogshit stomping away. Zeke threw the wrench against a car door. Barney muttered, "You shouldn'ta said that, Zeke. Not that you'd kill him."

Zeke gave them a cold stare. "Who heard me?"

"Not me," Chicken Salad said. "Sumabitch, I didn't hear shit."

"Me neither," Barney said.

Zeke glared up and down the line, his hands still shaking with rage.

Dogshit returned quickly with the super, both men red-faced with anger above their white shirts and dark ties. Clarence Hill stood behind them in a lavender shirt and white tie, shaking his head with disgust.

The three shirt-and-ties walked up the line and Zeke followed, his muscles tight with tension. Jerry saw them walking by. He flipped up his helmet and gestured questioningly, but Zeke was too angry to notice.

"This better not slow down your line, Miller," the super muttered over the clamor, sending a chill through Dogshit and making him bite his lip.

Zeke followed them into the Green Room. Clarence shut the door, killing some of the pounding noise. The small room contained only a long metal table with folding chairs. Everything was painted pale green and covered with dirt. Dogshit Miller and the superintendent sat on one side of the table, Zeke Brown on the other. Instead of sitting beside Zeke, Clarence Hill took the chair on the end and sat between them.

"Okay, Zeke," Clarence said. "What is it?"

Zeke glared at Dogshit and said, "I do my job and nobody can say different. I was my own man when I came and I'll be my own man when I leave."

"Which will be soon," Dogshit muttered.

"Okay," Clarence sighed, motioning for them to calm down. His job was to resolve these things at the lowest possible level. "Sounds like an everyday misunderstanding to me. Now Zeke'll buy Miller a bottle of Cutty and we'll all forget it happened."

"I ain't buying shit," Zeke said, glaring angrily at Clarence. "And you're worse than him. You ain't shit for a rep."

"Maybe you shouldn't be in this union," Clarence muttered, clenching his fists to repress his hatred.

Zeke returned his cold stare, knowing he'd have to force him into taking any action at all. Fucker wore a different uniform but played on the same team as the goddamn company.

"There you have it, Clarence," the super said. "You can see for youself. You can't even keep your own man in line. What I wanna know is if the union's gonna hassle us when we let him go."

"The union takes a hard line on firing," Clarence said. "Bald Eddie will want a hearing."

"Let's call him," Zeke said, knowing it would scare Clarence into action.

"We will not allow a foreman to be threatened," the super said. "That's the company's bottom line."

"Right," Dogshit said. "This shit's gotta be stopped. Half the men carry pieces as it is. There was a shooting at Dodge Main just last week—right on the line."

"It's really *not* that serious," Clarence said, knowing he couldn't lock out Zeke on this one. "Things just got a little out of hand. What do you say, Zeke? Do you see a way out of this?"

"Miller's been riding me," Zeke said. "I should get some consideration."

"Okay," Clarence said, seeing his chance at a quick resolution without involving Bald Eddie. He'd have to let Zeke and the super put the squeeze on his friend Dogshit. "Okay, Miller'll buy Zeke the Cutty and we'll all go back to work."

The super indicated that the company would pay for the bottle of Scotch and Dogshit said, "Okay."

"What do you say, Zeke?"

"Okay," he said grudgingly.

"Good," Clarence said, standing up. "It's all forgotten then. Shake hands and go back to work."

Dogshit stood up and extended his hand. "I ain't your enemy, Zeke. It's just my job."

Zeke stood up and shoved his hands in his back pockets. "If it's forgotten, there's nothing to shake about."

"That's right," Clarence nodded. "Let's get back to the line."

Zeke strode back down the line, nodding to Jerry that he hadn't been fired. Clarence, Dogshit, and the super headed the other way, grumbling among themselves.

Chicken Salad and Barney stopped working to watch Zeke return.

"Sumabitch, what happened, Zeke?"

"Got me a bottle of Cutty."

"Sumabitch."

"You did right, Zeke," Barney said, "If I didn't have eighteen years, I woulda done the same thing."

Zeke reached for his glue brush, then stopped and glared at Barney, his anger rushing back with full force. "You fucking hypocrite!"

"Huh?"

"If whitey wanted to fuck your ass, what would you do? Drop your pants and bend over?"

"Wha—?"

"Go off in the corner, just you and him?"

"I-I-I'd kill him."

"No, you already told me! You'd do anything to protect your eighteen fucking years! What makes you think your eighteen are more important than my seven? What makes your kids more important than mine?"

Barney stared at the floor, unable to move.

Seeing his devastated look, Zeke shuffled his feet, then put his hand on Barney's shoulder and said quietly, "Ah shit, forget it, Barney. It ain't even you I'm mad at."

Smokey had been watching from the frame-welding section. He walked over and pulled Zeke aside. "Lighten up, brother. This ain't no time to get funky."

"What do you mean?"

"I just saw the newspaper. The union's agreed to pay the money."

"No shit!" A sly smile crept slowly across Zeke's face and he slapped Smokey's outstretched palms with a loud smack.

The whistle blew for coffee-break time. Laughing together, they walked up the line and told Jerry.

His eyes popped open with excitement as he slapped their palms. "The whole thing! They're gonna pay the whole ten grand?"

"Hey, keep it down, sucker. You wanna tell the world?"

"Jesus," Jerry whispered, "I never even *seen* that much money. That's over three thousand each. At one time."

The three men strolled toward the vending machines, grinning together like kids on Christmas morning.

10

The union hall was packed for Bald Eddie's visit. The auto workers were angry and unruly as they listened to Clarence Hill read the official statement from the podium.

"The total was just over twenty thousand dollars, men. To be exact, twenty thousand six hundred."

Flannigan shouted, "Why's the union got so much cash?"

"Well, we were just holding it temporarily. From Local 682's strike fund. Somebody musta known."

Bobby Joe shouted, "Why don't you protect your money? The paper says the safe was wide open!"

The crowd grumbled in agreement.

"That's not exactly right," Clarence said, struggling to maintain control. "You see, uh—"

Bald Eddie stepped confidently to the podium.

"It wasn't *our* money, men. It was *yours*. They stole your money."

Zeke jumped to his feet and shouted, "Now you're talking! How we gonna get it back?"

"It was all insured," Bald Eddie said reassuringly.

"But what about the guys that did it?"

"Don't worry, Zeke. We've got nothing to worry about, men. The culprits will be caught. The police owe this union a few favors. In addition, we're putting up a thousand-dollar reward."

Zeke gestured to the crowd as if saying, "That's my man, Bald Eddie."

As Zeke sat down, Bald Eddie restored order and went into the details. It took him only fifteen minutes to satisfy the crowd and send them streaming out of the hall toward their cars.

A mini-cam TV crew met the workers at the door. The reporter shoved a microphone at their faces as they stepped into the fading sunset light.

"Tell me, sir. What do you think of the Oreo robbery?"

Bobby Joe shrugged. "Who cares? No skin off my ass."

"What *do* you care about?"

"The line. What else?"

"Yeah," Hank shouted, stepping in front of the mike. "Why don't you tell about that? How they'd rather pay me for a broken back than fix the machine that done it!"

The young reporter approached the next two workers striding through the door, anxious to get less controversial comments.

"What do you think of the Oreo Gang?"

"Fuck you, Jack," Smokey said without breaking stride.

"How about you, sir?"

"Fuck off," Jerry said.

The reporter glanced around, desperately searching for anything that could be broadcast. The camera was running out of film. He spotted a stoop-shouldered old worker, ran to catch up with him, and said, "Excuse me, what do you think of the robbery?"

"Sumabitch," Chicken Salad muttered. "I don't know shit."

"Yes, but are you satisfied with what the union's doing?"

"Sumabitch. Do you know Archie Bunker?"

Hank interrupted again and grabbed the mike. "I'll tell you the real shit. Listen to me! The goddamn line is so—"

The reporter tried to grab back his mike, getting into a tug-of-war with Hank and shouting for his crew to stop the camera.

Smokey and Jerry walked down the street to Smokey's candy-red Continental.

"We gotta think about the switch," Smokey said.

"Let's go to Oogie's. I gotta get home soon."

They opened the doors and climbed into the front seat. Suddenly Jerry spun his head around and stared at the stranger sitting in the back seat. He was a small Puerto Rican man in his forties, wearing sunglasses and a well-tailored three-piece suit. Jerry glanced at Smokey, but Smokey's face was expressionless.

"My name's Hernandez," the man said. "Charlie T. Hernandez. Smokey knows who I am."

Smokey nodded.

"You boys owe me some money."

"The papers got it all wrong," Smokey said, leaning over the seat with a worried expression. "There wasn't no ten grand, Charlie T. We paid you fair. It's all an insurance scam by the union."

"I don't wanna hear no stories, Smoke. I just want my grand. Or is it two grand?"

They followed Charlie's eyes as he looked across the street at his dark-blue Cadillac limousine manned by a tough-looking chauffeur in a dark uniform.

Smokey said, "We got something else, Charlie. Some stuff the union wants. Stuff they'll pay for."

"Yeah," Jerry said. "Just give us a couple weeks."

"What kinda stuff?"

Jerry said, "Illegal loan lists in—"

Charlie T.'s ears perked up, as Smokey shut up Jerry with a jab in the ribs and said, "Just stuff."

"Okay," Charlie T. said, backing off slightly. "Smoke and me go way back, so I'll give you a couple weeks. Smoke always pays his bills."

"That's right, Charlie. The union, you know, they say they'll give us the bread. But what if they don't?"

"You'll find it. You'll find it even if you hafta sell this car. You know that, don't you, Smoke?"

"Yeah. I know, Charlie."

Smokey and Jerry watched Charlie T. step out of the car, carefully straighten his suit, and walk slowly to his limousine.

"Jesus," Jerry groaned. "Carries a gun, don't he?"

"Fucking little spic carries everything."

"You handle it," Jerry said, reaching for his nasal spray. "I don't even wanna *see* it, Smoke. Don't want nothing to do with no slime-ass killers."

Smokey nodded, started the motor, and pulled away. They drove to Oogie's without talking and met Zeke at their regular table.

The bar was crowded after the union meeting, so they decided to talk outside. They each took a bottle of Stroh's and walked around the building to the parking lot. Leaning against the tavern's cinderblock wall, they sipped their brews under the spray-painted graffito saying, *White is Wonderful.*

"Dammit," Zeke said. "If those fuckers are gonna claim twenty grand from the insurance company, then we should ask for the same thing."

"Yeah," Smokey nodded. "But Charlie T. gonna get two thousand then, cuz I don't wanna mess with that little spic. He'll fuck you good."

Chicken Salad and Hank came out of the bar and waved as they walked toward their cars. "Take it easy, Zeke," Chicken Salad shouted.

"You too, Salad."

They waited until the two men drove off, then Zeke said, "How we gonna get the bread?"

"I don't know," Smokey said.

Jerry almost dropped his beer. "What the hell? I thought you had everything figured out, Smoke!"

"Making a switch ain't easy."

"We can use a locker at Greyhound," Zeke said.

Smokey shook his head. "They'd grab us picking up the money."

"Hell, not if they're afraid of the book," Jerry said.

"Yeah," Smokey nodded. "That's what we gotta find out. How much they want the book. Or if they're just playing games with us."

"Jesus," Jerry groaned. "Don't even say that shit. I don't wanna hear about no goddamn games."

Zeke's quick eyes flashed along the smoggy skyline, stopping on the Ford tower in the River Rouge plant. He already had a plan. "Look," he said, "we can rip the book in half, put half of it in a coin locker and ask for the money."

Bobby Joe staggered out of the bar with two other workers. As he headed for his car he shouted, "Hey, Jerry! You gonna play ball tomorrow?"

"Yeah, see you there."

They waited for the three cars to drive away, then Smokey said, "This ain't no good."

"It'll work," Zeke insisted. "We'll have them send the locker key to a post-office box."

"No," Smokey said, "I mean it's no good for us to be seen together like this. They know the job was pulled by two blacks and a white guy. We can't be walking around like a goddamn Oreo."

"Jesus," Jerry groaned. "What the hell we gonna do?"

"We're gonna do what we gotta do," Smokey said. "We talk by phone. We stop being seen with each other."

Nobody said a word. Zeke and Jerry glanced out at the dark twilight skyline. The parking lot suddenly seemed very quiet.

Finally Smokey tossed his beer bottle at the trash barrel. "Just go our own ways," he said softly. "If anybody asks, we just don't hang around together anymore."

They stood together in total silence. Each man stared down at his beer, realizing his life had just changed.

Jerry cleared his throat and said, "That's too bad. Arlene's gonna miss the bowling."

"Ah shit," Zeke muttered hoarsely, "you didn't take her that much anyway."

They leaned against the cinder-block wall for a long time, not moving, not talking. The last rays of daylight were fading over the distant Checker Cab plant. Each man began to face his memories alone and wonder what would come next. Nobody wanted to make the first move to leave.

Finally Smokey stood up, shrugged his huge shoulders, and said, "Well, I guess it's time to go."

Affectionately, Jerry slapped the palms of the two black men and said, "You crazy niggers take care."

"Same to you, you fucked-up honky," Zeke said.

Zeke and Jerry saw the pain in each other's eyes. They nodded to each other with stiff false smiles, as if they were grinning at some joke, unspoken and unspeakable.

Then the three grim-faced men turned away and walked in different directions toward their cars, their dim shadows drifting apart on the parking lot surface.

11

Three police officers spent the morning rummaging through a skid-row garage jam-packed with stolen merchandise. The walls were stacked with stereos and TV sets. Boxes were filled with cameras, typewriters, and sporting goods.

One officer catalogued the merchandise, while the other two interrogated the wrinkled old caretaker.

"Come on, Pop. Who's paying your bills?"

"I don't know nothing," the old man said, crossing his arms. "I just sit here."

"Yeah," the officer smiled, glancing at the hundreds of TV sets. "You just like to watch lots of TV, right?"

"That's right."

"Come on now. Who hired you?"

"I don't know."

"You better talk, Pop. This is gonna be a big rap to take alone."

By midafternoon the Detroit Police Department had their man in an interrogation room. He was Charlie T. Hernandez. The young detective grilled him, while the fat one watched.

"If you paid the old duffer a decent sum, he wouldn't have cracked. We got you dead to rights, Charlie."

"Amigo, I tink you got nothang, no?"

"Christ, Charlie. Would you stuff the accent?"

Charlie T. shrugged and examined his manicure.

The young detective leaned across the table and said, "You're making a mistake, Hernandez. There was a Harrington-Richardson .32 in the haul. A chrome-plated job. Ballistics says it was the gun that shot a police officer three weeks ago. He's still in the hospital."

Charlie T.'s face tensed, but he said nothing.

The fat detective said, "The old man says *you* brought in the box with the revolver. That makes you an accomplice."

Charlie T. leaned forward, dropping the accent. "Hey, man, you know I wouldn't have anything to do with a shooting."

"Do I? We got you this time."

"Okay," Charlie T. said. "I'll admit it don't look good. What can I trade? What do you wanna know?"

"Shit," the young detective sneered. "You ain't got nothing big enough to trade."

Charlie T. looked at him angrily. "What do you mean, I ain't got nothing big enough. You're talking to Charlie T."

"What you got?"

106

"I got three nobodies."

"So?"

"I got three nobodies who caught their little fingers in something bigger than they can handle." Charlie T. slouched back in his chair and grinned. "Something even too big for you boys. Something so big you'll have to hush it up."

"Like what?"

Bald Eddie Johnson received the information as he was getting ready to leave his office for the day. He stayed at his desk a long time. After quickly recovering from his initial surprise, he examined the union personnel files on Jerry Bartowski, Zeke Brown, and Smokey James. He read and re-read every word about the three.

His lawyer and bodyguard watched him without daring to speak. They could see he was still furious. But mostly he was eager to take action and just plain relieved to know at last who the hell he was dealing with.

Bald Eddie drank two cups of coffee while he stared at the three snapshot photos. He had to make the right move. He scrutinized the three faces with total concentration, searching for weaknesses.

Removing his glasses, he glanced at his lawyer and bodyguard for the first time in thirty minutes, saying, "Can you believe these guys?"

The two men shrugged sympathetically.

"We can't afford a single mistake," he said, picking up the three photos. "You never know what assholes like this might do. The dumb suckers ain't got much to lose."

The lawyer nodded and said, "Right, Eddie."

Bald Eddie showed them the photo of Jerry and said, "This one's a good union man. He'll buckle under a little pressure."

"Right."

Then he showed them the photo of Zeke. "This one's hungry. He wants a hand on the controls."

"Right, Eddie."

Finally he showed them the photo of Smokey. "This bastard's a two-time loser. He'll make us pay through the ass forever, then fuck us for the fun of it."

"Right."

"What do you think we should do?"

"What do *you* think, Eddie?"

Oogie's Bar & Grill was serving small groups of night drinkers. The Happy Hour crowd had gone home.

Smokey sat alone at the bar, nursing a beer near the pay phone. He knew he had to find a new place to hang out. He'd dropped in because it was Zeke's night to work overtime and Jerry's to pump gas. He glanced at their old table. It was empty. He thought of some women he might phone, but didn't feel like making the effort.

Instead, he watched the two middle-aged honkies seated down the bar in hunting jackets. He hadn't seen them before. They were heavyset like prize-fighters and looked almost like strong-arm thugs. But they were grumbling about doing night work.

A new kid from the plant came through the door and approached Oogie at the bar. "Hi, where's the john?"

"In the rear," Oogie said, pointing. "Use my name."

"Yeah, you'll get a good seat," Hank shouted.

Smokey glanced over at the table where Hank was sitting in his cowboy shirt, talking to Bobby Joe and two new black workers. Having found a new audience, Hank was doing the talking while the youngbloods bought the beers.

"That's right," Hank said, "they call themselves 'Mo-town' like, you know, Motor City. Made their money right here, still got a building down on Woodword Avenue. Berry Gordy, Diana Ross, and all them. Know where they are now? Yup, Beverly Hills. That's right. Living in big mansions and driving big limos. They got their asses outa here faster than you could say Su-premes. And you know who keeps buying their goddamn records which ain't got shit to do with Motor City? Yup, you and me. That's right. So Diana and Berry can piss away our money in Vegas."

Smokey turned away. He had just decided to get seriously drunk, when he heard somebody at the pay phone pretending to be from the phone company and asking some woman if her husband was home. It was one of the heavyset honkies from the bar, the taller of the two. He watched him hang up and return to his partner at the bar.

"He's at the gas station," the tall one said. "His wife's at home."

The fat one said, "You know how to get there?"

"Yeah. Let's go."

Smokey watched the two thugs chug their beers and walk out the door. He grabbed the phone, stuck in a dime, and dialed Jerry's number.

Hank spotted him and shouted, "Forget it, Smoke. She won't answer. She's got another man."

Smokey heard someone answer the phone, then said softly, "Hello. Arlene?"

"Yes?"

"This is Smokey James."

"Oh, hi."

"Did you just get a call?"

"Yes."

"From the phone company?"

"Yes," she said suspiciously. "They made a mistake."

"Are the kids there?"

"No, why? Is something wrong?"

"Well, uh, it's a little hard to explain. Uh, Jerry asked me to call," Smokey stalled, then suddenly knew what to say. "He just split his pants down at the station and wants you to drop off his extra pair. He's pretty embarrassed."

"Okay," she laughed. "Tell him I'll be right over."

Smokey hung up the phone and strode straight for the door. Oogie saw him and said, "Leaving early, Smoke?" But Smokey barreled out the doorway in too much of a hurry to hear anything.

Oogie gave Hank a puzzled glance. "What's with him? I guess she said yes, huh?"

"That's right, Oog," Hank laughed. "Must be one hell of a woman."

Smokey dashed across the parking lot, his legs straining, his eyes adjusting to the darkness as he reached his Continental. He flung open the trunk and grabbed his baseball bat, then quickly scrambled into the driver's seat, flashed on the headlights, and revved the huge powerful motor. Fuckers had a five-minute head start.

Burning rubber, he screeched away from Oogie's and gunned through a stoplight and screamed down the shortcut to the freeway. He lurched up the ramp, slammed the huge motor into overdrive and thundered down the freeway toward Jerry's neighborhood, roaring through the night at a hundred twenty, the exit signs flashing by like thrown knives.

Muthafuckers wanna play rough, he thought. Both sides can play that game, Jack.

He careened off the freeway, wheeled around the corner and slowed down. Jerry's tree-lined street was dark and quiet. He cruised slowly past the modest homes where windows glowed with the flickering light of television sets.

Smokey parked at the curb by the maple tree and carefully approached Jerry's front porch, the baseball bat dangling from his hand. The whole house was dark except for a small table lamp glowing dimly through the living-room curtains. He rang the bell and waited. Two dogs howled down the street. Nobody answered the bell.

Smokey jimmied open the front door and stepped into the dimly lit living room, then sat down on the stuffed sofa. He waited with the Louisville Slugger in his lap. Gonna rip the fuckers tonight, he thought. Who'd be shitface enough to beat on a guy's wife? Police, union, government? Don't make much difference. Be with that. Ratfuckers are all the same. Fuck your ass to death and make your survivors say thanks.

The doorbell suddenly rang, then rang again. The front door slowly opened. The two thugs stepped out of the darkness into the dim living room. Squinting, they spotted Smokey on the sofa and stopped in their tracks. They gave each other a puzzled glance and looked back at the sofa.

"Hi," Smokey smiled. "You boys looking for somebody?"

"I guess we got the wrong house," the fat thug said.

"No, you boys got the right place. Just the wrong time. Let's hear what you got to say."

The tall thug edged toward the door. The short one followed, saying, "Sorry to bother you. This is the wrong house."

Smokey jumped to his feet, strode across the living-room carpet, and followed them out the front door. The thugs saw him coming and broke into a run. They dashed across the front porch and down the steps. Leaping forward, Smokey swung the Louisville Slugger with one hand and clipped the short thug in the right ankle with a loud whack. The ankle bone snapped with a dull thud.

Stumbling, the fat thug sprawled across the front lawn, grabbing his broken ankle and groaning with pain.

Smokey stalked the tall thug around the front lawn, prodding him with the baseball bat and tapping his legs.

"Who sent you?"

They walked in circles around the lawn, barely able to see each other's eyes in the darkness. The tall thug glanced at his partner crumpled on the ground. Smokey began rapping his legs harder.

"Who?"

"Nobody." The thug kept backing away, struggling to jerk his arms and legs out of the path of the constant blows.

"Who! Tell me who, you redneck cracker!"

"Nobody, Mack. We just got the wrong place."

Smokey began swinging the Slugger with both hands and said, "I'm running out of patience, honky."

The thug dodged the heavy blows. Suddenly he pulled out a pocket knife and lunged at Smokey's throat, shouting, "Goddamn nigger!" Smokey blocked the blow and the thug raced for the sidewalk. Smokey raced behind him, strained to swing the bat, and clobbered him in the right leg, breaking the bone.

The tall thug tumbled onto the sidewalk and rolled over on his back, slashing his knife at the bat.

Smokey towered over him. "Who!"

The thug slashed at Smokey's foot and screamed, "Motherfucking coon! I'll kill you!"

Smokey lifted the Louisville Slugger above his head, and with all the power in his enormous arms smashed it down on the thug's left knee. The knee cap shattered with a sharp crack.

The thug yelped with pain, then passed out with his body slumped across the sidewalk, both legs twisted at odd angles.

The bat dangling from his hand, Smokey spun on his heel and strode back across the lawn to the short thug.

The short thug cowered with fear. He held up his hands and pleaded, "No more, brother. No more."

Smokey pointed his bat at the unconscious tall

thug and said, "You know he'll never walk again, don't you?"

"No more, brother."

"Don't you!"

"Yeah. Yeah, I know."

"You ready to talk yet? Who sent you?"

"Some union guy."

"What's the name?"

"I don't know."

Smokey prodded him with the bat. "The name?"

"He didn't say. Please, no more."

Smokey poked his broken ankle and said, "The name!"

"I don't know. Some guy who runs for Bald Eddie."

"That's name enough."

Dropping the bat, Smokey helped the short thug hobble to his Chevy and put him behind the steering wheel. Then he picked up the unconscious tall thug and gently loaded him into the back seat. Closing the door, he glanced at the short thug and said, "Don't drive too fast now."

The Chevy drove slowly down the street.

Smokey walked back to the porch, scooped up his Louisville Slugger and closed the front door. He was walking toward his car, when Jerry and Arlene pulled into the driveway.

They got out of their car and stared at him. Smokey was standing in the dark in the middle of their front lawn, a baseball bat dangling from his hand. Jerry walked toward him.

"What the hell's going on, Smokey? Is this some kinda joke?"

"Hey, Jerry."

"Jesus! You're bleeding." Jerry squinted at the

blood on Smokey's shirt. "What happened? Are you okay?"

"Yeah. It's from the other guys."

"Other guys? What other guys?"

"Who do you think?"

"Oh, Jesus, did Charlie T. come here?"

"Guess again, brother."

12

Zeke was nauseous from too much beer and groggy from too little sleep. He picked at his breakfast. All night he had dreamed about working glue-and-rubber like a good little boy, but Dogshit and Clarence kept shoving him into the pounding jaws of a sheet-metal cutter. He was struggling with his omelet, when Carolyn answered the phone and said it was Bald Eddie Johnson.

Zeke grabbed the phone, suddenly healthy and wide awake. Let him do the talking, he thought. Don't confess nothing, Jack.

"Hello."

" 'Morning, Zeke. How're you doing today?"

"Fine, Mr. Johnson."

"Call me Bald Eddie."

"How are you, Bald Eddie?"

"I've been thinking about your future, Zeke. I'd like to talk to you about it."

"Yeah. I think about it, too."

"Good. Can you meet me for lunch?"

"I gotta stay on the line, you know? How about after work?"

"I could give the plant a call, Zeke. I think you'll find this is more important."

"Yeah, okay."

"Good, Zeke. Do you know Denny's Steak House? It's near Cobo Hall."

"No," Zeke said slowly, remembering Jimmy Hoffa was last seen in a restaurant, "But I can go to your office. I could be there in an hour."

"Very good, Zeke. I'll be waiting."

Forty-five minutes later Zeke was seated in the office. He saw that Bald Eddie pretended to fiddle casually with a paper clip, but was really watching him like a hawk from the corner of his eye.

"I've been watching you for some time, Zeke," Bald Eddie said, propping his legs on his desk. "You remind me of myself when I was young. A little rough, a little pushy, you talk too much but you got guts. You're just the right guy to stand up for another worker's rights, Zeke. We've been thinking about what you—and other workers—have been saying about Clarence Hill. We think you're right. He's being transferred to a new plant in Ohio. I'd like you to fill in for him until the next election."

Zeke said nothing, wondering how much Bald Eddie knew and how far he would go. Stay cool, he thought. Don't take no sucker deals.

Bald Eddie lowered his legs, leaned forward, and looked straight at Zeke. "Now you can make those changes you've been talking about. The pay's six-teen-four a year."

"How much power am I gonna have?"

"How much can you handle?"

"Everything you got," Zeke said.

Bald Eddie stood up, walked around his desk, and sat in the chair beside Zeke. "If you can handle it, you can have it. This is a hard-ass outfit, Zeke. We don't take slackers."

"I'm no slacker."

"Good," Bald Eddie said, leaning close to Zeke's ear. "I think we're ready to make a horse-trade."

"I gotta think about this a couple days," Zeke said, rubbing his worried forehead.

"Of course. How much time will you need?"

"And I want assurances that Smokey and Jerry won't be hurt," Zeke said flatly, staring straight into Bald Eddie's eyes. "Not even a scratch."

"Of course."

"And assurances that they'll get their own compensations."

"Of course."

"I ain't jiving," Zeke said. He knew that Bald Eddie couldn't be trusted very far, that the only way to find out was the hard way, and that he had damn little choice. "This deal ain't going down, unless I get them assurances."

"No problem. That's my job. My job is to look after the welfare of each and every member in this union."

Their eyes met, the two men measuring each other's strength in the dead silence of the office.

"I want your word, Eddie. Your solemn word."

"You got it, Zeke."

The assembly line had stopped for the Friday afternoon coffee break. Two young workers sat against the wall by the vending machines, sharing a joint of marijuana. Above their heads a spray-painted graffito read, *Breathing Here 40 Hours a Week is Work Enuff!*

Hank, Barney, and Chicken Salad sat around the nearby table, drinking paper cups of coffee spiked with bourbon. The marijuana smoke drifted across their table.

"These youngbloods don't even know *how* to eat shit," Chicken Salad muttered. "Using them funny cigarettes. Sumabitch, we used to get disciplined for smoking regular cigarettes."

"That's right," Hank muttered. "Three disciplines —what a joke. These punks rack up nine and they still don't get laid off."

Barney nodded. "You hear about the kid in batteries? Just walked off midshift. Never came back for his half-week paycheck."

"Yup, that's right. And that kid Hemzacek who's always sick? He'll be here today cuz it's payday, but he's always sick Mondays and Tuesdays. Dogshit called his doctor and the doc says, 'Sure, for five bucks I'll say anything you want.'"

"Five bucks? Sumabitch, we oughta get a doctor like that."

Zeke stood in the locker-room doorway, staring at his coffee and thinking about Bald Eddie. Jerry spotted him and walked casually past, motioning for him to follow. They walked down the line and stopped where the others couldn't overhear them.

"Listen," Jerry said, nervously glancing around,

119

"I know we shouldn't be seen together, but I'm getting really worried. You hear what happened last night?"

"What?"

"Bald Eddie's ass-kickers, man. They came right to my house."

"Yeah, I heard," Zeke nodded. "Don't worry, man."

"Don't worry! What the shit, Zeke? I got monster men in my living room and you say don't worry. What the hell's gonna happen next? I'm getting scared."

"Just don't worry. I mean it, Jerry. Bald Eddie's gonna be cooled out. Charlie T.'s already on ice. And we ain't gonna hafta deal with no rollers neither."

"You kidding?"

"It's gonna work out."

Suddenly they both noticed Dogshit and Clarence coming out of the Green Room and walking along the other side of the line toward the coffee-break tables.

"Shit," Jerry muttered, moving behind a forklift.

Zeke lowered his voice and said, "We gotta have a meeting."

"Yeah," Jerry whispered, seeing Dogshit and Clarence look at them from across the line. "But where and when? I'm really scared."

Zeke glared back at Clarence, then whispered, "Tomorrow's Saturday. Come to my house in the afternoon. I'll tell Smokey."

Dogshit and Clarence saw the two men move from behind the forklift in opposite directions. They turned their heads, watching Zeke amble toward the windshield section.

Dogshit shook his head, saying, "This coming Monday? Zeke's gonna be the new rep?"

"Yeah," Clarence muttered bitterly.

"Are you serious? In charge of the whole salami? Zeke Brown?"

"Yeah, the jerk-off muthafucker."

"I don't believe it," Dogshit said, shaking his head again. "He's got a discipline sheet a mile long, Clarence. Damn near killed me just this week."

"You better start believing it, Miller. Monday you're gonna have his nigger ass right in your face."

"God damn."

"That smart-ass nigger's gonna shit all over you."

"Gotta be some way to get around this."

"Forget it, Miller. The way Bald Eddie talks, you'd think he was in love with the muthafucker."

"God damn."

"I'll see you at quitting time. Don't forget that work assignment for Smokey James."

"Yeah, see you later."

Dogshit walked into the coffee-break room and barked at the workers slouching around the tables and vending machines. "What the hell's going on here? Thirty seconds, men."

"Sumabitch."

He sniffed the air and said, "Who's smoking them funny cigarettes again? Let's get moving, boys."

"We're moving, Miller. We're moving."

The workers trudged back to their positions. The line rumbled back to life and began pounding at full roar.

Dogshit looked around for Smokey and found him coming out of the washroom.

"Good afternoon, Mr. Smokey James," he shouted cynically over the clamor.

"What is it now, Miller?"

"Clarence says they need a utility man next door. In paint room number three."

"Yeah."

Smokey headed up the line, watching the men at work. He spotted Jerry in the welding trench, spraying his nostrils. He saw Zeke on the windshield dock, grumbling at Chicken Salad. Gotta have a meeting, he thought. The switch still a bitch, but gonna be a *sweet* bitch. Fuckers are running scared. Book's driving them Looney Tunes. We can get more than the twenty, get some really *grand* grand. Get some of that *big* green. Gonna play it by the *book*. Be with that, Jack.

He opened a door near the end of the line and entered the adjacent building. It was cooler and less noisy. If it was ninety degrees outdoors, the paint building was only a hundred ten.

Smokey wandered around the building and located paint room number three. The small metal room was pressurized and had an airtight door. The coveralls, goggles, and gas mask hung from hooks on the metal wall beside the door.

He methodically pulled on the paint-spattered coveralls and tried to look through the small window in the metal door. But the windowpane was pebbled glass reinforced with chicken wire. He grabbed the wraparound plastic goggles and slipped them over his eyes, then glanced around the building to test them. The place was almost deserted. Just two guys loading paint drums. Other suckers were probably all in the parking lot, throwing dice for their paychecks again.

He picked up the black rubber gas mask,

strapped it over his nose and mouth, and made sure it was working. Turning the doorknob, he pulled open the metal door, then shut it behind him and closed the airtight lock. The small room was almost filled by a car frame painted undercoat gray. The air was thick with paint fumes.

Walking around the car frame, he checked the pressure gauge and started the twenty-second timer on the paint dial. The overhead nozzles suddenly sputtered and began traveling back and forth, spraying cobalt-blue paint on the gray frame.

The nozzles filled the room with noisy hissing and prevented him from hearing the forklift pull up outside the room and park smack against the metal door.

Picking up the paint gun, Smokey began adding the final touches to the car frame. After thirty seconds the car was completely cobalt blue. He walked over to the timer and saw the dial had not moved. He turned the dial off. But the nozzles continued spraying the room, the thick wet paint dripping off the car frame and spilling across the concrete floor. He switched the dial back and forth repeatedly, until it snapped off in his hand. Dogshit's gonna dock my pay for this, he thought. Fuckers never fix nothing till it breaks. Gonna dock me for the extra paint too, the bastards.

He reached angrily for the emergency button and jammed it down. The red light flashed on. But the nozzles continued spraying, filling the air with floating particles of blue paint. He pushed the button again and again, but nothing happened. Blue paint gushed off the car and streamed across the floor, forming thick sticky pools. Raising the paint gun, he pounded the emergency button until the whole emergency box popped off the wall and dropped to the slippery blue concrete.

Floating paint particles stuck to his goggles and smeared across the plastic, making the whole world suddenly turn into a vast ocean of cobalt blue suffocating and drowning him. He jerked off the goggles and felt his eyes sting and blur from the poison fumes. Squinting at an overhead nozzle, he leaped up and reached for the stop-valve, but slipped and tumbled to the floor, splashing into the thick blue paint.

Paint particles clogged the air vents in the gas mask and he ripped it off. Gasping for air, he gulped deadly fumes and particles into his lungs. Unable to stand, he crawled through the swirling blue paint on his hands and knees, gasping, coughing, spitting blue paint from his mouth. He reached the car frame and pulled himself to his feet, his bulky frame a solid cobalt-blue.

He braced himself against the car, feeling faint, his lungs screaming for air, the blue paint running into his eyes. Barely able to see, he carefully slid his blue shoes across the slippery blue concrete and staggered dizzily toward the metal door, gasping violently for air.

Reaching the door, he fumbled with the airtight lock and forced it open. He turned the doorknob and pushed, but the door would not move. Raging, he slammed the weight of his huge body against the door, but it didn't budge. Fuckers trying to kill me, kill me, kill me. . . .

Suddenly vomiting spasms shook his body, pitching him violently forward. His lungs wretched up a glob of blue paint stained with dark blood.

Almost passing out, he summoned all his strength and pounded his blue fists against the pebbled glass. Gasping, straining, he hammered and hammered until the glass cracked. He rammed his blue head through the broken glass and collapsed with his neck jutting out the window, his motionless face dripping cobalt-blue paint and dark-red blood onto the yellow forklift.

Two workers rushed forward, one quickly moving the forklift, the other opening the door. A cloud of blue paint burst out the doorway. Coughing, they dragged Smokey away from the paint room and into the main building, leaving a blood stained blue smear across the floor.

"Is he dead?"

Dogshit and the superintendent dashed into view and ran toward Smokey's body.

"Quick! Give him mouth-to-mouth," Dogshit shouted.

"Billy," the super shouted. "Get the ambulance! Quick!"

Dogshit dropped to his knees beside Smokey's blue face, placed his mouth over the wet blue lips, and began blowing air into the lungs.

"Shit," the super muttered, squatting beside Dogshit. "If he's dead, he's gonna die in the ambulance, Miller. Nobody dies in here during my shift."

13

Jerry tried to follow his usual Saturday morning routine. He sat at the kitchen table with his checkbook and ball-point pen, trying to figure out how much he could afford to pay on the bills that were the longest overdue. Everything seemed normal. Arlene was ironing in the living room. Bob was playing in the back yard. Debby was twirling her baton around the kitchen, her portable stereo blasting out "Seventy-six Trombones."

But Jerry could not concentrate. His mind drifted back eight years, recalling the day they'd all joined the plant—Jerry, Vince, and Jan, high school diplomas in their pockets, zooming up to the job application office on their matching motorcycles. Damn, they'd been cool. Six months later Vince

Lang was dead, squashed by four car frames that crashed from the ceiling when an overhead cable snapped. Squashed worse than a goddamn cockroach. Hell, you couldn't even find him. They had to scrape the pieces off the floor with shovels. Then Jan began staying home all the time except during hunting season, afraid to take a piss without his wife's permission. And now. And now Smokey was gone, the goddamn company medics tossing him in the ambulance like a slaughtered slab of beef. But this was different, dammit. Smokey's death was no accident. And that was only the beginning. Now it was just Zeke and Jerry, like two goddamn sitting ducks, like two goddamn cockroaches. Well, they weren't gonna squash Jerry Bartowski without a killer hellfire of a fight.

Jerry stared at his checkbook, suddenly feeling vulnerable and very alone. He glanced into the living room and shouted, "Arlene, come here a minute." Then he looked at Debby and gestured toward her noisy stereo. "Could you turn that down, honey? Daddy's trying to work."

Debby smiled at him with her new teeth braces, twirling her baton and saying, "Am I good, Daddy?"

He looked into her bright sparkling eyes and said, "You're beautiful, Debby. You really are."

"That's right, honey," Arlene said, walking into the kitchen. "Now why don't you practice in your room?"

"Okay," Debby said, grabbing her stereo and twirling down the hallway.

"What is it, Jerry?"

"I thought you were gonna go up to Manistee and see your mother?"

Arlene wrinkled her brow. "What are you talk-

127

ing about? That was last June. We didn't have the money, remember?"

"I've been thinking about it. Maybe you oughta go. Take the kids. They need a vacation."

Arlene sat down at the table, giving him a puzzled stare. "What *are* you talking about? The children are in school."

"You know what I'm talking about." Jerry put down his ball-point and stared at her. "I want you and the kids to get out of town for a while. Go to Manistee. Take the Greyhound."

"What's going on, Jerry?"

"Something funny with the union. I don't think you should be here."

"This doesn't have anything to do with Smokey's death, does it?"

"Maybe. Yeah, it does."

"You didn't have anything to do with that, did you?"

"No."

"Then what is it?"

"I can't tell you."

"Jerry, what's going on?"

"Don't ask, Arlene. Just get the kids and start packing."

"Right now? Can you tell me what—"

Jerry stood up and started for the back door. "I'll drive you to the station. If we hurry, you can catch the noon bus and be there before dark. I'll get Bob. You call your mother."

She watched him walk out the door and began biting her nails.

Zeke gripped the railing of the pedestrian overpass, staring down at the Saturday morning traffic

128

on the freeway and waiting for Bald Eddie. He had insisted on holding the meeting in a place from which he could easily escape.

He tapped the railing with his clenched fists, recalling the day Wilson died three years before. They'd been skintight since high school. Wilson was one slick dude, always trying to sign a singing contract with Motown. But his shoe got caught in a sheet-metal press, sucking him in between the huge steel rollers. By the time they shut the huge machine off, the steel rollers had run up over his legs and arms to his chest, pressing him flat as a piece of paper, his blood gushing out the bottom. Only thing sticking out of the steel rollers was his head and upper chest. Dogshit ran up and said, "You got less than five minutes to live, Wilson. In a minute the numbness'll wear off and you're gonna start screaming. You got any final messages?" Wilson smiled and said, "Turn the muthafucker back on, Dogshit." Died inside the steel rollers, died like he'd become a piece of company property, like he'd become just another hunk of goddamn machinery. And now Smokey. Smokey was the same, lying in the hospital bed with his mouth all full of blood and paint. Fuckers were worse than killers. The killing wasn't enough. Fuckers painted him like he was just another goddamn machine, like he was just another piece of company product, just another hunk of goddamn junk plopping off the assembly line. Well, the muthafuckers weren't gonna turn Zeke Brown into another one of their goddamn machines. No way, Jack.

Suddenly he noticed Bald Eddie approaching with a hulking bodyguard. They walked to the middle of the overpass and stopped in front of Zeke. The bodyguard stood behind Bald Eddie.

"You lied to me," Zeke snarled.

"What?"

"You killed Smokey, you muthafucker!"

"Be careful who you call a murderer, Zeke."

"What the fuck do you call it!"

"I've been in meetings all night and morning," Bald Eddie said calmly, trying to be reasonable. "It's a case of extreme negligence, possibly criminal negligence."

"Negligence, my ass! Fuck your negligence! That's bullshit and you know it!"

Zeke clenched his fists and moved toward Bald Eddie, ready to bust his ass and throw him off the overpass.

The bodyguard quickly stepped forward, thrusting his hand inside his coat toward a shoulder holster.

Zeke stopped and slowly lowered his fists, saying, "Two can play that shit, Jack."

"You need a quick education," Bald Eddie said angrily, growing red in the face and jabbing his finger at Zeke as he spoke. "I came up this union the hard way. When I was your age, there was no forty-hour week, no sick benefits, no retirement pension, and no blacks at all. These changes happened because people like me knew when to look the other way. More changes can happen if you do the same."

"You had Smokey killed."

"So what? Who cares? Five hundred blacks were killed in Detroit last year alone. That's ten dead niggers a week. Who remembers? Who cares? Every year there's one hundred thousand industrial deaths in this country. That's four hundred dead workers every workday. Nobody remembers. Nobody cares."

Zeke stood with his fists clenched at his sides, his eyes burning with hatred. He glared at Bald Eddie and said, "You killed my friend."

"You thought it was gonna be easy to be a union rep. Well, now you know. It's rough and it's dirty. I thought you had the guts to be a shop steward. Maybe you do. Maybe you're one of those guys who knows when to look the other way, but remembers and cares."

Zeke's eyes blazed; his innards churned with hate.

"You've got two choices, Zeke. You can be stupid and get dead like your friend, or you can be smart and make changes like you want."

"You had this all planned. Didn't you, you muthafucker?"

"Zeke," Bald Eddie said, his voice becoming calm again. "Whether you hate my guts or not, what I'm telling you is still the truth. The straight facts of your situation."

"Yeah, and the fucker who put me in this situation is you."

"Believe whatever you like. The job is still yours if you want it. What I want is your answer."

Zeke glanced down at the endless stream of cars, the Fords and Chevys and Chryslers zipping along the Motor City freeway.

Jerry drove Arlene and the kids to the Greyhound Station and put them on the noon bus to Manistee. Then he got in his car and quickly drove away. He couldn't stand to see Arlene with tears in her eyes, carrying on like she was never gonna see him again or something. Women were always crying about the most stupid silly shit. Hell, the last time he cried was when the Detroit Tigers won the World Series.

He drove past the modest houses on Zeke's street and parked at the curb. Zeke's kids were playing ball on the sidewalk. He waved to them, walked onto the front porch, and rang the doorbell.

Zeke opened the door and stepped outside, signaling that they would talk on the porch.

"I don't want Carolyn to hear this," Zeke said.

"Yeah."

They walked to the end of the porch and glanced at each other, not knowing where to begin. Jerry sat on the railing. Zeke leaned against the house.

"You look tired," Jerry said.

"Yeah. So do you."

"Didn't get much sleep. I'm getting really scared."

"Yeah," Zeke nodded. "It sure is a mean mutha-fucker."

"Hell, we both know Smokey was murdered. It wasn't no fucking accident like the company says."

Zeke nodded.

"What we gonna do about it?"

"Nothing can help Smokey now," Zeke muttered, grimacing with pain.

"Our friend's been killed. I don't like doing it, but we hafta expose the union. Like you said."

"It's not that simple, Jerry."

"What do you mean?"

"We can't expose them without going to jail ourselves."

"Maybe we can make some kinda deal with Burrows, the F.B.I. man."

"You crazy? How we gonna live to tell about it?

This shit is for real, Jerry. These muthafuckers are mean."

"What about the notebook?"

Zeke glanced at the street, his voice cold and serious. "I said it wasn't that simple. Things've gotten complicated."

"You mean you don't have the notebook?"

"Our local is on the edge of a revolution. There's gonna be some big changes. We're gonna shake it up, Jerry. I've been waiting for this all my life."

"Waiting for what?"

"I'm taking Clarence's job. I am the new rep."

"Jesus! You gave it to them."

Zeke looked at the street, then saw his kids and shouted, "Ali, get on the sidewalk! You play in the street and you're gonna get killed. You never know who might drive by."

The boys trudged back to the sidewalk,

"You gave them the notebook, didn't you?"

"There was nothing *really* illegal in it. Well, illegal, but not wrong. The union was just trying to make a little extra money for our pension fund."

"You dumb asshole. You think those bastards'll let you change anything? They just bought you off with a promotion."

"No. They may *think* they bought me off, but they bought a stick of dynamite. I'm gonna tear hell in this union."

Jerry groaned and stared at his feet, then looked at Zeke and said, "What about Smokey? Was that legal? What we gonna do about that?"

Zeke winced and muttered, "Dogshit Miller's being fired for negligence."

"That don't mean shit. Hell, it wasn't even *his* fault."

BLUE COLLAR

Zeke walked to the front door, then walked back to Jerry. "Look, sucker, what's better? Going to the pen for a cat who's already dead or staying free so you can make some changes? It's a club in my hands, and I'm gonna use it."

Jerry groaned and turned his head.

Zeke put his hand on Jerry's shoulder. "You're my friend, Jerry. But you're *still* white."

"What the fuck does that mean?"

"Means you got more chances than me. Always did, always will. Black man gotta kiss one white ass or another. At least I can choose which ass I'm gonna kiss, and I ain't gonna choose one that'll shit in my face. At least I gotta chance to change things inside the union. To help the brothers."

Jerry stood up and shouted, "Fuck changes. Fuck your revolution. Fuck the brothers. I'm looking out for Number One. What's in it for me?"

"What do you want? They never woulda paid us."

"The union gets the notebook, you get promoted to a soft job and—"

"Now wait just—"

"Okay, okay," Jerry muttered bitterly. "Okay, you get the chance to change things. But what do I get?"

"They need a foreman to replace Dogshit. I'll get you the job."

Jerry turned his head away in disbelief, muttering, "I get screwed. That's all I know."

They both stared at the black kids playing ball. The two men stood side by side on the porch, not moving, not talking, grimacing with pain and tension.

134

14

Jerry parked his old gray Ford by the riverbank, glanced across the water at Windsor, Ontario, and unlocked his glove compartment. Taking out his Smith & Wesson .38 revolver, he loaded five of the six chambers. Then he tucked the pistol under his belt and pulled his shirt over it. Bastards try to get me and they'll get a goddamn war, he said to himself.

Getting out of his car, he strolled onto the old bridge connecting downtown Detroit with Belle Isle. He leaned against the railing and stared across the river at the Windsor skyline gleaming in the fading afternoon sunlight. Damn, he thought, I'm in this cold mutha all by myself. I'm freezing in ice up to my ears and they're trying to tell me it's summertime.

Shortly before sunset John Burrows stepped onto the bridge and walked toward Jerry. He stopped beside him and propped his elbow on the railing.

"Hello, Bartowski."

Jerry said nothing.

"The shit's coming down," Burrows said calmly. "I suppose you know that. We didn't find out until after the union did. The Detroit Police Department don't keep secrets very well. This is a company town."

"Yeah," Jerry muttered with a bitter laugh.

"Why didn't you come to me first, Jerry? I could have prevented all this."

"I didn't have anything to do with it."

"You can still help us get Bald Eddie."

"I got nothing to sell," Jerry said flatly. "I helped steal a notebook. I heard some conversations. I saw an industrial accident. Only two people can back me up. One's dead. The other's a union rep."

"Let us worry about that, Jerry. We'll piece it together."

"What do I get out of it?"

"Knowing you did the right thing."

"Shit," Jerry muttered disgustedly.

"A suspended sentence."

"Big fucking deal. How do I protect my family?"

"You got no choice now. I'm the only one that can protect you or your family."

"Fuck it," Jerry mumbled, staring across the river at Windsor. "Maybe I'll go to Canada. It can't be any goddamn worse over there."

"They'll find you wherever you go," Burrows said quietly.

"I can take care of myself."

"Can you? Is that why you carry that roscoe?"

Burrows poked at the revolver under Jerry's shirt. His voice became flat and hard. "Face it, Jerry. You're one man all alone. You're black friends won't help you now."

Jerry stared at the running waters of the river, knowing Burrows was right. But what the hell, you don't betray the union to outsiders, no matter what. Without your union, you had nothing at all.

"I'm giving it to you straight," Burrows said quietly. "Without me, you're one man all alone in this."

"I won't help you, Burrows. I'd let them kill me before I turned stoolie."

"Will you?"

"I just can't do it."

"You really think you owe them your life?"

Jerry spun on his heel and strode along the bridge toward his car, staring at the tubular towers of Renaissance Center and the bleak jagged skyline of Detroit. Nighttime was stealing across the dark buildings, the chilling darkness stretching from the Chrysler assembly plants in the Polish American neighborhoods of Hamtramck all the way to the Ford assembly plants in the Black American neighborhoods of River Rouge.

Zeke sat in his living-room chair, broodingly polishing off his second six-pack of Stroh's.

Carolyn was watching TV with the kids. She kept glancing at Zeke with a worried frown. He was never so quiet and still in the evening.

Finally she said, "Are you going to Smokey's funeral?"

"Yeah," he muttered.

"Is it tomorrow?"

"Yeah."

"If you want me to go, I should call Mary right now. To see if she can watch the kids, you know?"

"I'll go alone."

"Is Jerry taking Arlene?"

"Carolyn," Zeke said flatly, "I don't wanna talk about it."

"Okay, honey," she said sympathetically. "Those accidents are always so awful. I'm just grateful it didn't happen to you. I remember when it almost happened to my father."

Zeke stared at his beer.

"At least things are looking up for us," she said, trying to snap him out of his morbid silence. "Your promotion should cover the heating as well as the taxes, won't it?"

Zeke glared at her angrily and said, "Carolyn, I said I don't wanna talk about it."

Jerry was alone in his house. At nine o'clock he turned out the lights and dropped on the bed with his revolver tucked in his jeans. He was exhausted from the tension, but still couldn't sleep. He lay in the darkness for a long time, staring at the ceiling. Suddenly he heard a noise in the yard. He bolted out of bed and looked out the window, but couldn't see or hear a thing. Bastards are hiding, he thought. Waiting for me to make a mistake.

He tiptoed to the closet and took out his Winchester 12-gauge shotgun. Fumbling in the darkness, he located the ammo box and stuck two shells in the chambers. Then he walked quietly into the dark living room.

He sat on the sofa with the shotgun at his side. He sat perfectly still, listening for the slightest noise. The lights from the house across the street shone through the curtains. The only sound was his tense breathing. He sat in the darkness for thirty minutes, until the tension made his head buzz with his father's drunken gripes about there being no way out. Screw this shit, he thought. I gotta get outa here and make the bastards try to find me.

He stepped quietly into the kitchen and looked at the clock. It was only five minutes to ten. He threw on a jacket, cautiously entered the garage, placed his shotgun in the back seat of his old Ford, then got behind the wheel and backed into the street, one hand gripping the revolver in his belt.

He drove down the street, turned onto Route 41, and headed for Oogie's Bar & Grill, constantly checking the rear-view mirror. Bastards probably gonna bust into the house at dawn, he thought. Try to catch me asleep.

Pulling into the dark parking lot, he got out and locked the car. He checked to be sure the revolver was hidden under his jacket, then glanced around and walked through the doorway into the tavern.

Hank and Bobby Joe motioned for him to join them, but he just nodded, went to the stool at the far end of the bar, and sat with his back to the wall.

Jerry paid Doris for a beer and bourbon, then glanced around the room carefully. Nobody looked suspicious. The only stranger was already drunk. Oogie was playing pinball with Bobby Joe. Two youngbloods were shooting pool. Dogshit was seated at the middle of the bar, staring drunkenly at his whiskey and bitching to Doris, saying over and over, "It just ain't fair, Doris." Hank was talking with Flannigan.

"That's right," Hank said. "But how'd he ever get to be the new rep? Just tell me that."

"You know how it is, Hank. They gotta give these blacks whatever they want."

Jerry stopped listening, paid Doris for another round, and stared at the bourbon, his fingers nervously drumming on the bar. He gulped down the bourbon and sipped the beer, then glanced at their old table. Three empty chairs. I'm the last of the Oreo Gang, he thought. Dead last. Jesus, I gotta slow down on the bourbon. This is no time to get shitfaced. Fuckers are just waiting for this.

He began biting his thumbnail and watched Dogshit return to the jukebox. Dogshit punched the same song three times again, staggered back to his bar stool, and hunched over his drink all alone, listening to Merle Haggard sing about getting laid off at the factory.

At eleven o'clock Jerry stuck a dime in the pay phone and called Manistee collect. When Arlene answered, he could hear "Seventy-six Trombones" playing in the background.

"Arlene? It's me."

"How are you, Jerry?"

"How are *you?*"

"Fine."

"Is there anything unusual?"

"Like what?"

"Salesman or guys hanging around or anything?"

"No. This is a small town and it's almost midnight."

"Where are the kids?"

"They're here."

"Don't let them go out alone."

"What's wrong, Jerry?"

"I think they're following me."

"Who?"

"I'm the only one left, Arlene. I'm the only one who knows what went down. About the notebook, the loans, Smokey's death, how Zeke got his job. Everything will be okay when I'm dead."

"I should be there," she said urgently. "Where are you now?"

"At the bar. I'm afraid to go home."

"Call the police right now."

"I'm not a brave man, Arlene. I can't take them all on."

"Can't you get a job like Zeke did?"

"Yeah, but I don't trust them."

"If you just keep quiet, won't they leave you alone?"

"I don't see how they can."

"Oh, honey."

"Jesus. Don't cry, Arlene. I'm gonna be fine. I'll call you tomorrow."

Jerry hung up and walked back to his bar stool. *If they touch her or the kids, I swear to God I'll kill them all.*

At two o'clock Oogie unplugged the pinball machines and shouted, "Drink it up, fellas. Closing time."

The late-night stragglers headed for the door.

Jerry finished his beer and watched the TV mounted over the bar. Brando was bleeding and struggling toward the warehouse in *On the Waterfront*. He remembered watching it when he was a kid and still thought a man could do more in life than kiss ass and fight just to keep kissing.

Doris turned off the TV and looked at him.

"Come on, Jerry. Time to go. What's wrong? Got troubles with the wife again?"

Jerry nodded goodnight and headed toward the

door, wondering if he should go home. Hell, maybe the bastards won't do anything. Screw that. Bastards had done worse over smaller shit than this.

He strolled slowly across the parking lot and glanced at a maroon Chevy parked in the far corner, then stopped and squinted more closely in the darkness. He was sure he'd seen two guys in the front seat, ducking down when he looked at them. With his hand on the revolver he walked quickly to his car, started the motor, and flipped on the headlights. He slowly edged his old gray Ford across the lot and onto Route 41, closely watching the Chevy in the rear-view mirror. Ten seconds later the maroon Chevy pulled out of Oogie's and followed him. Jesus, that's them. Fuckers been waiting in the lot.

Gripping the steering wheel, Jerry turned down a side street, then drove through an alley behind darkened used-car lots. The Chevy's headlights followed, fifty yards behind. Feeling his scalp tighten, he flexed his shoulders to stop the cold shivers running down his spine. Fuckers gonna kill me.

Terrified, he gunned the Ford along the shortcut, lurched onto the eastbound Chrysler Freeway, and pushed the straining motor up to eighty miles an hour as he raced toward downtown Detroit. The headlights followed, staying a hundred yards behind. He was urging his overheated engine up to ninety when, suddenly, the maroon Chevy roared up beside him. He glanced out his side window and saw the guy in the back seat stick a high-powered deer rifle out the window.

Jumping with fright, he turned the wheel,

ducked down, and kicked the accelerator to the floor. His heart pounding frantically, he desperately pumped the speedometer up to a hundred as his panicky eyes peered over the dashboard to keep from crashing into the guardrails. He tried to look in the rear-view mirror but didn't dare lift his head. Hunching up his shoulders, he shot a fast glance out the side window, saw the Chevy had moved, and ducked down again, the sweat gushing down his taut trembling face. Suddenly his hands shook with violent jerking spasms. Straining, he squeezed the steering wheel with white knuckles and gradually steadied himself, then peered again over the dashboard at the streaking freeway blur. He pumped the accelerator furiously, but the rattling overheated motor made the whole car tremble. Finally he screwed up enough courage to lift his head and take a quick look in the rear-view mirror. The Chevy was thirty yards behind him.

He jerked the .38 revolver from his belt and gripped it with his right hand while clenching the wheel with his left. Reaching the end of the freeway, he careened down the ramp and barreled through the deserted Civic Center at a hundred miles an hour. He ran six stoplights rocketing down Ford Avenue and barreling through the backstreets of Corktown. The Chevy stayed right on his tail.

Slewing onto Michigan Avenue, he thundered through twelve stoplights on Skid Row. Everything was a rainbow haze of streetlights, stoplights, and neon lights. In back was solid darkness and the two piercing headlights.

Suddenly a blue-and-white police car pulled out of an alley and blocked both lanes twenty yards in front of him. He jammed on the brakes. The old Ford fishtailed, spun around, slid sideways, and crashed broadside into the squad car, showering the street with broken glass.

The police officers crawled from their mangled squad car and staggered toward him.

Jerry shot a glance through his shattered window and saw the maroon Chevy making a U-turn and trying to get away. He suddenly realized the two guys were his only proof the union was trying to murder him.

Jerry tromped down the accelerator and screeched after the speeding Chevy. He hurtled through deserted back streets, twenty yards behind them, smoke belching from his screaming engine. The two cars roared and twisted along the Detroit River at ninety miles an hour when, suddenly, they saw a roadblock around the curve, three police cars thirty yards away. The Chevy tried to swerve around them, but sideswiped a squad car, bounced over the curb, and smashed head-on into a telephone pole. Slamming on his brakes, Jerry skidded over the curb and crashed into the rear end of the Chevy.

Police swarmed over the damaged cars with their revolvers drawn, dragging the two guys from the Chevy and clicking on handcuffs.

An officer ripped the revolver from Jerry's hand, slugged his bleeding face, and jerked him out of the car. Another officer slammed him against the car and snapped on handcuffs. His face was forced up at the neon sign reading, *Tunnel to Canada*.

"I wanna confess a robbery," Jerry said, spitting blood.

"You gotta hear your rights."

"I wanna confess, but I'll only talk to an F.B.I agent named John Burrows."

"You have a right to remain silent. You—"

"It's about a murder."

15

Zeke and Jerry wanted out, but there was no out. Like most men, they labored in a workaday world where the lines were sharply drawn and never to be questioned. Unlike most, they had found the lines to be falsely drawn, leaving them free to draw their own. But even this was not an out. Without the old lines they didn't know where or how to draw the line, and the workaday world never gave them an opportunity to find out.

Ten days after his arrest, Jerry Bartowski was riding with John Burrows in the back seat of an unmarked F.B.I. car. Burrows instructed the agent who was driving to cross the huge parking lot of the auto plant.

The F.B.I. car passed the job application office

and drove slowly along the long drab wall of the assembly building, then stopped near a small door.

Jerry stepped out and glanced around in the afternoon sunlight, nervously recognizing the parked cars of his former day-shift co-workers. He wore a blue plaid sport shirt and brushed cotton jeans. He walked to the doorway and entered the pounding clamor, protected by an F.B.I agent on each side.

The two agents followed as he walked down the line toward the locker room. Jerry spotted Jenkins and started to wave his hand, but Jenkins took a step off the line, shouting over the noise, "You asshole scab!" Several men stopped working as he walked past, spitting disgustedly or shouting insults.

Bobby Joe shouted, "Stoolie! Goddamn stoolie!"

Chicken Salad sneered, "Big sumabitch man!"

Hank strode down the line, barking proudly in his new job as foreman. "Back to work, men. That's right, keep it rolling. This ain't no floor show."

Jerry entered the locker room, opened his locker, and as the agents watched, began quickly stuffing his baseball glove, tattered work clothes, and bottles of medicine in his gym bag.

Zeke Brown was talking with the super in the Green Room, demanding better ventilation and more skilled jobs for blacks. He wasn't a shirt-and-tie. He wore a brown silk shirt with matching dacron pants. He was bringing up the lack of safety inspections, when Hank stuck his head through the door and told the super about Jerry.

"That's right, he's here right now."

"Where?"

"Cleaning out his locker."

Jerry stepped out of the locker room and saw

Zeke waiting for him near the line. They exchanged angry glares. Then Jerry walked past Zeke without saying a word.

Zeke said to his back, "I'd hate to live in your shoes, you scum fink."

Stopping, Jerry turned and stared at him. Someone hit the button, stopping the line. The workers gathered around, watching Zeke and Jerry edge closer to each other, both men boiling with rage.

When they were only six feet apart, Jerry said, "I see they finally fixed your locker."

"You don't give a fuck about your fellow workers, do you, you dumb Polack? Just save your own ass."

"You're the one who double-crossed me," Jerry snarled through gritted teeth, clenching his fists. "You tried to get me killed."

"Do anything to keep outa jail," Zeke mocked, his trembling face barely containing his violent rage. "Sell your white ass to the police!"

"I ain't the one that sold out, you nigger shit!"

Zeke leaned closer, clenched his fists, and shouted, "Fuck you, whitey! You're just another goddamn white boy looking out for hisself, don't give a fuck about anybody else!"

"You goddamn nigger!"

"I ain't forgetting you, honky! You gonna have to move to another city, hide your children—"

"Nigger!"

"Asshole whitey!"

Jerry leaped forward, thrusting his stocky body against Zeke's wiry frame and ramming his knee into Zeke's groin. Zeke buckled forward, then quickly hauled back and smashed his roundhouse right into Jerry's face, cracking the bone and sending blood spurting.

Jerry spun around, grabbed a power wrench, and raised it like a billy club. Zeke quickly scooped up a power-drill and cocked his arm, wielding it like a blackjack. Burrows grabbed Jerry while Hank pulled back Zeke. But the two raging men thrashed free. Their eyes blazing with a murderous hate beyond control, their powerful muscles straining, their faces contorted with rage, they lunged forward.

Someone shouted, "Kill him!"

Jerry Bartowski and Zeke Brown swung at each other's skulls, ready to bash out each other's brains, ready to take the life of a friend. Both had forgotten the words of Smokey: "Everything they do, the way they pit the lifers against the newboys, the black against the white, is meant to keep us in our place."

There they stood, Zeke Brown and Jerry Bartowski, the lust for murder in their hearts, the will to murder in their eyes, the tools of murder in their hands. Yet they didn't look like murderers. They didn't look like killers at all. They looked like Americans.

SPECIAL OFFER: If you enjoyed this book and would like to have our catalog of over 1,400 other Bantam titles, just send your name and address and 25¢ (to help defray postage and handling costs) to: Catalog Department, Bantam Books, Inc., 414 East Golf Rd., Des Plaines, Ill. 60016.

ABOUT THE AUTHORS

LEONARD SCHRADER attended Calvin College, studied
fiction at the Iowa Writers Workshop, and taught at
Doshisha and Kyoto Universities in Japan. He has written the novel and film story for *The Yakuza*.

PAUL SCHRADER attended Calvin College, studied film at
UCLA, and was editor of *Cinema* magazine. He is the
author of *Transcendental Style in Film* and has written
the screenplays for *The Yakuza, Obsession, Rolling
Thunder* and *Taxi Driver*. *Blue Collar* is the first film he
has directed.

DON'T MISS
THESE CURRENT
Bantam Bestsellers

☐	11001	**DR. ATKINS DIET REVOLUTION**	$2.25
☐	11580	**THE CASTLE MADE FOR LOVE** Barbara Cartland	$1.50
☐	10970	**HOW TO SPEAK SOUTHERN** Mitchell & Rawls	$1.25
☐	10077	**TRINITY** Leon Uris	$2.75
☐	10759	**ALL CREATURES GREAT AND SMALL** James Herriot	$2.25
☐	11770	**ONCE IS NOT ENOUGH** Jacqueline Susann	$2.25
☐	11699	**THE LAST CHANCE DIET** Dr. Robert Linn	$2.25
☐	10422	**THE DEEP** Peter Benchley	$2.25
☐	10306	**PASSAGES** Gail Sheehy	$2.50
☐	11255	**THE GUINNESS BOOK OF WORLD RECORDS 16th Ed.** McWhirters	$2.25
☐	10080	**LIFE AFTER LIFE** Raymond Moody, Jr.	$1.95
☐	11917	**LINDA GOODMAN'S SUN SIGNS**	$2.25
☐	2600	**RAGTIME** E. L. Doctorow	$2.25
☐	10888	**RAISE THE TITANIC!** Clive Cussler	$2.25
☐	2491	**ASPEN** Burt Hirschfeld	$1.95
☐	2300	**THE MONEYCHANGERS** Arthur Hailey	$1.95
☐	2222	**HELTER SKELTER** Vincent Bugliosi	$1.95

Buy them at your local bookstore or use this handy coupon for ordering:

Bantam Books, Inc., Dept. FB, 414 East Golf Road, Des Plaines, Ill. 60016

Please send me the books I have checked above. I am enclosing $_____
(please add 50¢ to cover postage and handling). Send check or money
order—no cash or C.O.D.'s please.

Mr/Mrs/Miss_____

Address_____

City_____State/Zip_____

FB—3/78

Please allow four weeks for delivery. This offer expires 9/78.

Bantam Book Catalog

Here's your up-to-the-minute listing of every book currently available from Bantam.

This easy-to-use catalog is divided into categories and contains over 1400 titles by your favorite authors.

So don't delay—take advantage of this special opportunity to increase your reading pleasure.

Just send us your name and address and 25¢ (to help defray postage and handling costs).

BANTAM BOOKS, INC.
Dept. FC, 414 East Golf Road, Des Plaines, Ill. 60016

Mr./Mrs./Miss_____
                    (please print)

Address_____

City_____State_____Zip_____

Do you know someone who enjoys books? Just give us their names and addresses and we'll send them a catalog too!

_____

Mr./Mrs./Miss_____

Address_____

City_____State_____Zip_____

_____

Mr./Mrs./Miss_____

Address_____

City_____State_____Zip_____

FC—6/77